A SPECIAL KIND OF MAN . . .

There were three of them. When one of them grabbed for Sherry, I didn't waste any time. I flicked my wrist and Hugo jumped into my hand. I slashed Sherry's assailant's face, kicked the other man and cut the last one deeply on the thigh. They shouted something to each other and then took off.

"Why didn't you shoot them, you could have killed them!" Sherry remarked.

I frowned at her, wondering what she was getting after. "I could have, why are you asking?"

With thrill in her eyes, Sherry replied, "I think you're a very dangerous man!"

NICK CARTER IS IT!

"Nick Carter out-Bonds James Bond."
—*Buffalo Evening News*

"Nick Carter is America's #1 espionage agent."
—*Variety*

"Nick Carter is razor-sharp suspense."
—*King Features*

"Nick Carter is extraordinarily big."
—*Bestsellers*

"Nick Carter has attracted an army of addicted readers . . . the books are fast, have plenty of action and just the right degree of sex . . . Nick Carter is the American James Bond, suave, sophisticated, a killer with both the ladies and the enemy."
—*The New York Times*

FROM THE NICK CARTER
KILLMASTER SERIES

APPOINTMENT IN HAIPHONG
ASSASSINATION BRIGADE
BEIRUT INCIDENT
THE CAIRO MAFIA
CARNIVAL FOR KILLING
CAULDRON OF HELL
CHESSMASTER
THE CHRISTMAS KILL
THE DAMOCLES THREAT
DAY OF THE DINGO
DEATHLIGHT
THE DEATH STAR AFFAIR
THE DEVIL'S DOZEN
DOCTOR DNA
THE DOMINICAN AFFAIR
DOOMSDAY SPORE
THE DUBROVNIK MASSACRE
EARTH SHAKER
THE GOLDEN BULL
THE HUMAN TIME BOMB
THE HUNTER
THE INCA DEATH SQUAD
THE ISRAELI CONNECTION
KATMANDU CONTRACT
THE LAST SAMURAI
THE MENDOZA MANUSCRIPT
NORWEGIAN TYPHOON
THE OMEGA TERROR

OPERATION: McMURDO SOUND
THE OUSTER CONSPIRACY
PAMPLONA AFFAIR
THE PARISIAN AFFAIR
THE PEMEX CHART
PLEASURE ISLAND
THE PUPPET MASTER
THE Q MAN
THE RED RAYS
THE REDOLMO AFFAIR
REICH FOUR
RETREAT FOR DEATH
THE SATAN TRAP
SIGN OF THE COBRA
THE SNAKE FLAG CONSPIRACY
SOCIETY OF NINE
SOLAR MENACE
THE STRONTIUM CODE
THE SUICIDE SEAT
TEN TIMES DYNAMITE
TIME CLOCK OF DEATH
THE TREASON GAME
TRIPLE CROSS
TURKISH BLOODBATH
THE ULTIMATE CODE
WAR FROM THE CLOUDS
THE WEAPONS OF NIGHT

A Killmaster Spy Chiller

NICK CARTER

THE GREEK SUMMIT

ACE CHARTER BOOKS, NEW YORK

THE GREEK SUMMIT
Copyright © 1983 by Condé Nast Publications, Inc.
All rights reserved. No part of this book may be reproduced in any
form or by any means, except for the inclusion of brief quotations in a
review, without permission in writing from the publisher.

All characters in this book are fictitious. Any resemblance to actual
persons, living or dead, is purely coincidental.

An Ace Charter Original

Published by arrangement with Condé Nast Publications, Inc.

"Nick Carter" is a registered trademark of the Condé Nast Publications, Inc., registered in the United States Patent Office.

ISBN: 0-441-30272-6

First Ace Charter Printing: February 1983
Published simultaneously in Canada

Manufactured in the United States of America

Ace Books, 200 Madison Avenue, New York, New York 10016

*Dedicated to the men of the
Secret Services of the
United States of America*

PROLOGUE

"I will not have a government lackey following me around everywhere I go, General," Doctor Lucas Johns, a tall bespectacled man in his early forties, spoke the words with disdain.

"Now, Doctor, please—" the general started, but the doctor wouldn't hear any argument against his statement.

"That's my final word on the subject, General," Johns said emphatically.

The general, white-haired and almost a full foot shorter, wished now that he had retired long before he'd ever met Doctor Lucas Johns. He looked over at the doctor's wife, hoping for some assistance, but Sherry Johns offered no help in trying to convince her husband to accept a government assigned bodyguard. A voluptuous brunette former showgirl, Sherry didn't understand her husband's business—and didn't care to.

"Doctor," the general tried again, striving to make his tone more commanding, "you know that we can't allow you to attend this summit without the proper protection."

"Then I won't go," the doctor replied. "That's a simple solution, isn't it? I really have no desire to attend any summit meeting and share my knowledge with a bunch of Third World, second-rate scientists."

"Doctor, we are sharing this knowledge with other governments as a show of good faith, and to attempt to keep the balance of power."

"Screw the balance of power, General!" Johns shouted. "This entire concept was mine from the very beginning."

"There are other scientists, Doctor, who feel that they have modifications that could improve—"

"My designs cannot be improved on!" Johns shouted again, slamming his fists down on the desk. "Not unless I improve on them myself!"

"All right," the general said. "I'm not going to argue that with you. You've already agreed to go, all I'm asking is that you take one specially qualified man with you."

"Specially qualified?" Doctor Johns said with heavy sarcasm. "No, General."

"Look, Doctor, let's compromise," the general suggested, playing his last card.

"Compromise?"

"Hire your own man."

Johns hesitated a moment, as though he'd had intentions of arguing with whatever the general was going to say, but now had second thoughts.

"What?" the doctor asked, looking very interested.

"Hire a private detective to go with you," the

general said. "The government will pay the freight—"

"No, no," Johns said, waving his hand, looking thoughtful. "I can pay my own bills."

Johns looked down at the astrology chart on his desk and said, "That's a very good idea, General. In fact, it's an excellent idea."

"You can't argue with—What?" the general asked, not sure he'd heard right.

"I said it's a good idea, General," Johns said, patting the smaller man on the shoulder, solicitously.

"Uh, yes," the general said. "Well we can suggest someone."

"Oh, no," Johns replied, "no suggestions. I'll hire my own man. That way I'll *know* that I am getting my own man. Agreed?"

The general hesitated, then shrugged and said, "Agreed."

"Yes," Johns went on, pulling a telephone book from the bottom drawer of his desk, "a very intriguing idea, indeed."

He turned to the appropriate page in the Washington phone book and stopped right at the top name.

"Son of a—" he said, and then snatched up the telephone and began to dial. "Hello," he said, "is this the Aries Detective Agency?"

The general put his hand over the lower portion of his face to hide his satisfied smile, and at the same time let out a sigh of relief.

ONE

From the moment my boss, David Hawk, told me that he had a nice easy one for me, I expected trouble. Eyeing him warily, I sat in front of his desk and waited for him to elaborate.

"Do you know who Doctor Lucas Johns is?" he asked me.

"Sure. He's a brilliant scientist working for the United States, specializing in weapons research."

"We're sending Doctor Johns to a summit meeting for top scientists from all over the world. They're supposed to exchange information on whatever projects they're working on, and Doctor Johns resents having to go and share his knowledge with what he has called 'a bunch of Mickey Mouse scientists.' He feels that he's infinitely superior to any other scientist in the world today."

"Is he right?"

Hawk hesitated a moment, and then said, "From all indications, yes. In any case, Johns is not making an aspect of this trip easy for us. In fact, he was being most difficult in the matter of having a bodyguard with him at all times during the meeting. He refused to accept a government assigned man—which would have been you."

"So then, why am I here?"

"We've devised an alternate plan," Hawk said. He opened the top drawer of his desk and took out a large brown envelope.

"What's this?" I asked, accepting it from him.

"In there you will find a passport, a private investigator's license and other documents, all identifying you as one Nick Diamond, employed by the Aries Detective Agency here in D.C."

"You had all of this set up in advance?" I asked, examining the photostat of my investigator's license, which appeared to be—and very likely was—quite real.

"We did."

"How did you know that Johns would call this particular detective agency?" I asked.

"Doctor Johns is a firm believer in the stars," he explained. "Reads his horoscope religiously every day, has his charts done—all of that business that has to do with astrology. When we checked the telephone book, it seemed a logical assumption that he would look no further once he encountered the name 'Aries,' which was listed first."

I replaced everything back in the envelope and put it in my lap.

"So then there is actually such a company."

"Oh, yes, very definitely," Hawk said. "It is, in fact, actually a one man operation, but we have arranged with the, uh, owner to allow you to represent him in this matter. Naturally, all fees will go to him."

"Naturally. What's his name?"

"Amos Weatherbee."

"And are we partners, or am I an employee?"

"Play it any way you feel it's necessary, N3," he said. "I doubt that the doctor will call and check on you with Mr. Weatherbee, but you are covered if he does. This is Doctor Johns' address," he added, handing me a slip of paper. "Please don't say or do anything to antagonize him, N3. He is supposed to approve of you and give you the job."

"Of accompanying him to the summit meeting."

"Correct."

"Where's it being held?"

"In Greece."

I raised my eyebrows. "Nice work for a private eye, if you can get it," I commented.

"That is your job, N3," he said.

"What is?"

"To get it."

TWO

The door to Doctor Johns' home was answered by a man I suspected was a Federal agent; a butler wouldn't have frisked me.

"I'll hold the gun until you leave," he said, sliding Wilhelmina from my holster.

Normally, I wouldn't have objected, but Johns appeared to be a rebel, and an argumentative one at that. If he was going to hire himself a private eye, he'd want one with the same qualities. Johns didn't like government men, and if I didn't get along with this one, that would improve my chances of impressing the doctor. As Hawk had said, my assignment was to earn his approval and get the job.

"Tell Doctor Johns I was here and I went home," I told the agent, holding out my hand for my gun.

"What?"

"You've seen my I.D., friend," I said. "You know who I am, and you know that I was sent for. What more do you need? Tell the doctor that if you take my gun, I go home. That's it."

He compressed his lips in annoyance and said, "Wait here," and left me standing in the foyer.

A few minutes later I heard the doctor's voice. "I told that general I didn't want any government idiots," he was saying. "Of all the stupid—you knew I sent for this man . . ."

He calmed down as he approached me and immediately returned my gun. "I'm sorry, Mr. Diamond," he said, shaking my hand. He had incredibly long fingers, but a firm grip. "Would you follow me, please?"

"Doctor Johns?"

He was well over six feet tall and very thin. He was wearing black frame glasses with thick lenses, and walked with a slight stoop.

"Yes, I am. Follow me please?"

I tucked Wilhelmina back into my shoulder holster and gave the agent a triumphant look. As I followed the doctor, I was sure the man was staring daggers at my back, but I didn't turn around to verify it.

Johns led me to a small office in the back of his house, and closed the door behind us. We were not alone, however.

The woman in the room stood up as we entered. She had long legs and good breasts, and looked to be in her late twenties. Her sex appeal was not contrived, which had probably served her well as a showgirl, but I wondered how it served her in her life as the wife of an eminent scientist.

"Darling, this is Mr. Diamond," he introduced

us. "Mr. Diamond, this is my wife, Sherry."

"I'm happy to meet you, Mrs. Johns," I said, taking her hand. She looked me up and down appraisingly, and I wondered if her husband noticed.

"A pleasure, Mr. Diamond," she replied.

"Sit down, Mr. Diamond," Doctor Johns said, seating himself behind his desk.

I sat in a straight-backed chair directly across from the doctor, and his wife sat on a small sofa against the wall to my right.

"I suppose you're wondering what it is I want to hire you for, Mr. Diamond."

"I understood that it was a bodyguard job, Doctor Johns," I replied.

"Oh, it is, but it's a little more than just that. Do you know who I am?"

I shrugged, saying, "You're a scientist and you're very important to the government, as I understand it."

"That's true. Is that all you know?"

"That's enough, isn't it?" I asked. "As long as you can pay my fee, that's plenty."

He liked that, and laughed.

"Yes, I can pay your fee, Mr. Diamond, have no fear of that," he assured me.

"If you're so important to the government, doctor, why aren't they picking up the tab?" I asked.

"Because I want you to be in *my* employ, Mr. Diamond. Let me explain a little further what the job entails."

"Please do."

"The government is sending me—forcing me, in fact—to Greece for a meeting with so-called 'scientists' from other countries. We are supposed to compare notes and such, although I can't imagine what they could have to tell me that I would be interested in," he said, shaking his head. "In any case, the government tells me that while I am there I will be running the risk of possibly being kidnapped or even assassinated."

"That makes sense."

"Yes. Well, they wanted to send one of their men, probably an idiot, like the man at the door—"

"Lucas, darling . . ." his wife said, warningly.

"Yes, I know," he said to her, smiling warmly. "My wife thinks I should be more tolerant," he said to me. "In any case I refused to have this government dolt accompany me on the trip, and so I decided to hire my own bodyguard."

"Me," I said, another indication that I was paying attention.

"Correct. What are your politics, Mr. Diamond?" he asked.

"Nonexistent."

"Excellent!"

"I couldn't hope to make a living in this town if they weren't, Doctor Johns," I explained.

"Interesting," he said. "Well, then, I would like you to accompany my wife and myself to Greece and keep us safe from any kind of harm. That is the job, Mr. Diamond, in a nutshell."

"I accept," I said.

"Good. How soon can you start?"

"I have a suitcase in the trunk of my car, Doctor. I can start immediately."

"Excellent," he said, satisfied. "Then we can release that idiot outside and he can inform his boss that you are on the job."

"That's fine."

"I'll go and tell him," Johns said, standing up and walking around his desk.

"Doctor, would you mind if I asked how you came to choose our agency?"

"Not at all," he answered. "It was in the stars, Mr. Diamond," he said, obviously greatly pleased with his answer, "it was in the stars."

THREE

The agent refused to leave the house without calling General Davies. While he was on the phone I went out and got my suitcase from the trunk of the car. When I came back in the agent was listening intently to his boss and he didn't look happy. As he hung up he threw me a malevolent glare, and then left the house without speaking to any of us.

"Sore loser," I said to no one in particular.

"Come, Mr. Diamond," Sherry Johns told me, "I'll show you the guest room."

"Fine," I said, picking up my suitcase and following her, "but I would also like to see your bedroom . . ."

"Really?" she asked, looking at me over her shoulder.

"As well as the rest of the house," I went on.

"Oh," she said, and I couldn't see her face as she turned away again, "of course."

"Where is Doctor Johns?" I asked when we reached the guest room.

"Oh, he's in his office, buried in his work, no doubt," she told me.

"Did I notice that there were no windows in his office?" I asked her.

"Yes, you did," she said. "The government insisted on that."

"Very smart," I said, throwing my suitcase on the bed. "Shall I unpack?" I asked her. "When is this trip to Greece?"

"Actually, we'll be leaving tomorrow afternoon, so I suppose there's no point in unpacking anything but what you would need for tonight."

"Fine," I said, not bothering to open the suitcase at all. "Could you show me the rest of the house, now?" I asked her.

"Of course."

She gave me a tour of the house, which had seven rooms, a basement and two doors, one front and one back. The back was a good-sized yard with a patio and a garden, and high, concrete walls all around.

"Also at the request of the government?" I asked.

"Of course," she said. "I hate it. Makes me feel like I'm imprisoned."

"I can imagine."

"Would you care for some lunch?" she asked me.

I realized that I was hungry. "Yes, as a matter of fact, I would."

"Come with me to the kitchen," she invited.

"Will the doctor be joining us?" I asked as I followed her.

"No, Lucas doesn't eat lunch. I'm very used to

lunching alone, Mr. Diamond," she told me, "and it will be a treat to have someone to eat with, for a change."

"The pleasure will be mine," I told her.

Over lunch she asked question after question about what it was like to be a private detective. I made up the kind of stories I thought she might enjoy hearing.

As she cleaned up our plates—lunch was some warmed-up, leftover stew which she had made the night before—she said, "You certainly seem to have lived a very interesting life."

"Well, most of the work is routine, but there have been some interesting moments."

"What about women?" she asked.

"What about them?"

"Are you married?"

"No."

"Have you ever been?"

"No."

"Why not."

My answer was truthful. "Marriage doesn't go with my line of work. I've known some fine women in my life and I've had some nice relationships, but I would never subject a woman to the rigors of being married to me."

"That sounds very . . . unselfish," she commented.

"I don't know about that," I said.

"No, take my word for it, it is."

"All right," I said, "if you insist."

"Coffee?"

"Please. How long does your husband usually stay in his office?" I asked.

"Most of the time," she said. "It would be very easy for you to protect him if we didn't leave this house, because nine times out of ten, you would find him in there."

She poured two cups of coffee and then sat down at the table with me again.

"Doesn't sound like a very exciting life for you," I said.

"It's not," she agreed, "but I've had excitement in my life."

"On stage?" I asked.

She looked surprised. "How did you know that?"

"I did some checking after your husband called us yesterday," I lied.

"I see. I guess you are a detective, aren't you?" She sipped some coffee and then went on. "Yes, you're right. Being on stage was exciting, until I realized that I would never be much more than a member of the chorus line. I had the looks, I know that," she said, quite frankly, "but I was a little too short on talent."

"That's very honest," I told her. "I'm impressed."

She looked as if she might blush and said, "I've always tried to be honest—at least, with myself—so that I would never be all that disappointed."

"Do you miss it?" I asked. "Being on stage?"

"Sometimes," she said, "but Washington is a

stage. There are certain social functions that Lucas' position dictates we attend, and when we walk in I'm on stage, on display, all over again."

"I understand," I said.

"Do you want to ask me now why I married someone like Lucas Johns?"

"It hadn't occurred to me."

"I'll tell you, anyway," she said. "He was kind, considerate, attentive, and he wanted to marry me, so I said yes."

"And goodbye to the stage."

"Lucas told me I could still perform on stage if I wanted to, but that wouldn't look right," she said. "It wouldn't do him any good, so I retired."

"That's rather unselfish, too, isn't it?" I asked.

She smiled at me and said, "I don't know about that."

She was a very desirable woman and in that small kitchen, at that small table with our knees almost touching underneath, I was acutely aware of that fact.

"You're an odd man," she said, suddenly.

"Why do you say that?" I asked.

"You're not what I pictured a private detective as being," she said. "You seem to be too intelligent."

"Thanks a lot," I said.

"That's not what I meant," she said, quickly. "I meant that there are obviously other things a man like you could be doing."

"I guess it all comes down to that fact that I

like doing what I'm doing," I told her.

"That makes you very lucky," she said.

She took the empty cups to the sink and I watched her as she rinsed them out. There wasn't an ounce of spare flesh on her. Her breasts and hips seemed to be just the right size, and her waist was incredibly slim. She was wearing a skirt, and her legs were long and lovely.

She turned and caught me studying her and she leaned against the sink and looked right back at me. I think we both liked what we saw, which put us in a very explosive situation.

"I think I would like to walk around the outside of the house," I told her. I stood up and said, "Thanks very much for lunch, Mrs. Johns."

"You can call me Sherry, Nick," she said, still watching me.

"Uh, if you don't mind, I think I'll just continue calling you Mrs. Johns."

"That's fine with me, but I intend to continue calling you Nick," she told me.

"You can call me whatever you like, Mrs. Johns," I told her. "Your husband is paying for that privilege. Excuse me."

On that formal note, after a very informal lunch, I left the kitchen to check out the grounds.

FOUR

Johns came out of hibernation for dinner, and during that meal Sherry Johns was totally silent while her husband went on and on about everything and anything. I listened politely. I tried like hell to keep my eyes off Sherry Johns, but I don't think her husband would have noticed if I'd been staring at her hungrily or in distaste. He was too intent on keeping up his constant line of talk. I thought that this was perhaps a byproduct of his locking himself in his office for most of the day. It all had to come tumbling out, sometime.

Finally, he spoke about the trip to Greece.

"It's ridiculous," he said. "It's like sending me to a meeting of shoemakers and asking me to explain nuclear fission."

"You don't have very much regard for your colleagues from other countries, I gather."

He snorted. "The very thought that there's anything any of them could teach me is preposterous," he said.

"Then why go?"

"Because the government wants me to," he said, "and the government funds all of my research. If I could find independent funding, you can bet I wouldn't be going."

"And neither would I," I said.

"Good point."

I found the relationship between Johns and his wife to be a strange one. There was no evidence of affection, other than the spoken endearments which seemed to come more out of force of habit than any real feeling. Also, there was no touching between the two, not even the small things that usually pass between a couple in love—a hand on a shoulder, fingers on the cheek, that sort of thing.

And then there was Sherry's total silence at dinner.

An odd relationship, to say the least.

"Tell me about the trip," I said to him at that point.

"We'll be flying out in the afternoon," he said, neglecting to mention time or airline. "At the airport in Greece we will be picked up by a car and driven to the point where the meeting will be held."

"Hotel, motel, private house?" I asked. "On an island, in the city?"

"You'll find out when we get there, Diamond."

Johns had seemed to settle on calling me Diamond. Nick was too informal, and "Mr." Diamond was too formal. I called him Doctor, and continued to call Sherry Mrs. Johns.

"Will I be able to accompany you anywhere

you go while in Greece?" I asked.

"Everywhere but the actual meeting room," he said. "No one will be allowed in that room but the attending scientists."

"I see. Will there be any objection to my standing right outside the door?"

"I don't know, Diamond. There will be a security team there, and we'll find out the arrangements when we get there. Sherry, I have some more work to do tonight. I'll see you both in the morning."

He got up and left the room, and I looked across the table at Sherry Johns.

"Once he gets rolling he can really talk, can't he?" I remarked.

"Yeah," she said, looking up at me and smiling awkwardly. "Would you like some coffee?"

"Sure."

"I'll bring it out on the patio."

"Good," I said, standing up. "I'll uh, wait . . . outside."

"All right."

I went out and sat on a patio chair, looked up at the moon and hoped I wasn't getting involved in anything more than a bodyguard job. Sherry Johns was a nice girl. Maybe she wasn't too bright, or maybe she just wasn't too bright *by comparison*, but she had put herself into that position and there was nothing I could do about it. I had the feeling that away from Doctor Lucas Johns, she would shine; but she was around him, and she kept herself under wraps.

I wished I could have seen her on stage, some time.

She came out with a tray bearing two cups of coffee and assorted cakes. She sat on the other patio chair and put the tray down on the small table between us.

"I guess we make a strange couple to people," she said, and then looked at me and added, "to you."

"Not my place to say," I replied, sipping my coffee and studying the moon—or what there was of it. Right then, it was just a sliver of white in the sky that I could have reached out and cut my finger on.

"Sure it is," she said. "You're entitled to your opinion."

"And you're entitled to yours," I told her. "So how come when the doctor is around, you never give your opinion?"

She looked away and said, "That's not why he married me."

"Oh, I see. When you married him you gave up your opinions, your individuality."

"You don't have any right to talk to me that way," she said.

"Sure I do," I countered. "I'm entitled to my opinion, remember?"

"Nick—" she said in a shaky voice.

"Yes."

She looked at me with moist eyes, but whatever it was she was going to say was lost in an explosion and the sound of shattering glass.

"Shit," I said, catapulting off the patio chair. Sherry was right behind me as I ran back into the house with Wilhelmina in my hand.

When we reached the living room we found that the front window of the house was gone, completely blown away. Lying in the middle of the living room floor was Doctor Lucas Johns.

FIVE

"I thought you were supposed to be protecting this man," General Walker Davies said viciously.

"Settle down," I told him. I wasn't even sure whether or not the general knew who I really was, but if he did—and I *thought* he did—he was the only one in the room.

The others were what Johns had called "the lackeys," Davies' crew, who were outside looking for some sign of who might have blown out the window of Johns' house with a shotgun. Johns had hit the floor to get out of the way, and that's where he was when Sherry and I had come running in.

"Don't blame my bodyguard, General," Johns said, walking over to us. "If I had stayed away from the window, this wouldn't have happened. Of course, it you people had given me someplace else to live, somewhere a little more isolated—"

"We've been through that, Doctor. We have a limited budget, and all of it is allotted to your work."

"Oh, yes, that's right," Johns said. "I forgot.

Does that mean that I have to pay for a new window out of my own pocket?" he asked, pointing to the large hole where his front window used to be.

The general got a pained look on his face and said, "We'll take care of the window, Doctor. In the meantime we'll secure it with some boards. I've assigned two men to remain outside the house overnight. Tomorrow I'll be here to escort you to the airport." The general then turned to me and asked, "Are you sure you didn't see anything?"

"I was out the front door as soon as I realized what'd happened, General. Whoever fired the shot was long gone."

The general looked at me and the doctor, and the same distasteful expression remained on his face.

When he left I told the doctor and his wife to bed down on the floor in his office.

"There are no windows," I said, "it'll be safer in there."

It seemed to me that the thought of both of them sleeping in the same room seemed to upset them.

"What if they just blast through the wall?" he asked, seriously.

"Or drop a bomb on the house from a plane?" I asked.

"What?"

"One is just as likely as the other, Doctor," I said. "Nothing else is going to happen tonight, but

I want you both in that room anyway. Understand?" He seemed about to protest but I added, "This is what you hired me for, Doctor."

"Yes," he replied, "I suppose it is." He turned to Sherry and said, "Come, my dear. Diamond is right."

"I suppose he almost always is," she said, but I don't think he heard her.

"And don't come out," I shouted after them as they went toward his office. "If you want a drink, or you want to go to the bathroom, call me. Understand?"

"We understand, Diamond," Johns said at the door of his office. "There's no need to speak to us as if we were children."

"Sure there is," I answered him, "because from now until this meeting of yours is over, I'm your daddy."

He stared at me, and then—almost reluctantly, it seemed—went into his office and shut the door.

I walked over to the boarded up window and checked out the floor in front of it. There was a little glass, ground up now from all the feet that had trampled over it. I opened the front door and the two men that Davies had left behind turned and looked at me.

"How you guys doing?" I asked.

They looked at me boredly and nodded.

"I just want to take a look . . ." I told them, and walked over to the boarded up window. There was a lot of glass lying around in the garden directly under it, and some in the lawn further out.

I turned around to go back inside.

"Everything okay?" one of them asked.

I turned and looked at him and said, "Yeah, fine."

SIX

Athens, Greece, is a unique city.

The heart of Athens is as modern and sophisticated as any other European country, but walk a few blocks in any direction and suddenly you're in the shadow of Ancient Greece, Rome, Sparta, Byzantium and treading in the wake of Aristotle and Sophocles. It's an intriguing combination of the modern and historic.

We had departed from New York early enough so that when we arrived in Athens, there was still some daylight left. Greece is seven hours ahead of New York time.

We were met at the airport by a contingent of American security men, in plain clothes.

"Doctor Johns?" one man asked, approaching us as we entered the terminal.

"That's right," Johns said.

"My name is Robinson. If you will give your tickets to one of my men, sir, your bags will be collected."

Johns handed over his and Sherry's claim

tickets. When I did the same, the security man frowned—first at me and then at Johns.

"Doctor," he said, "we understood that you and your wife—"

"Mr. Diamond is my personal bodyguard," Johns told the man. "I'd appreciate it if you would collect his luggage as well."

"And my gun," I added. I'd given my gun up in New York, with the understanding that it would be returned once we reached Athens.

"Your gun?" the security man asked.

I nodded.

The security man turned to Johns and said, "Doctor, we have a perfectly competent security force—"

"I'm sure you do," Johns said to him, "but I've brought my own man just the same. Would you collect our luggage, please, and Mr. Diamond's gun, so that we can get a move on? I'd like to catch some daylight during the ride to the hotel so that my wife can see some of the sights."

The security man tightened his lips, turned slightly red and then nodded to one of his men, who took my claim ticket and my gun permit.

The man in charge was about my age, tall and fit with a lot of pride in his job, and he didn't like me. He directed us outside and we waited while our luggage was collected and brought to the car.

They took us to the Kings Palace hotel, which was right next to the Tomb of the Unknown Soldier, both of which are right off Constitution Square, called Syntagma by the Greeks.

"My men will see that your luggage is taken to your room," Robinson said to Johns, and then in grudging deference to me, he corrected himself and said, "I mean, rooms."

"Thank you, Mr. Robinson. Shall we go inside, dear?" Johns said to Sherry.

"I'll go with you to check in, sir," Robinson said. He flanked the Johnses on the left while I walked on their right.

The lobby of the hotel resembled an old, classy ocean liner. It was all highly polished wood and high ceilings. All of the lobby furniture had a heavy, solid, very reliable look to it.

For a large hotel, the foot traffic was startlingly sparse. There was no turmoil of guests coming and going, or bellboys lugging bags about.

The desk clerk was speaking in French to the man ahead of us, and when we approached and he found we were American, he lapsed into fluent English very easily.

"We are very happy to have you staying with us, Doctor Johns," the clerk said. "You and your lovely wife," he added.

"I'll be needing a room for my associate," Johns told the clerk as he signed in.

"Certainly, sir. I'm sure we can find something for him," the clerk said obligingly.

"On the same floor," Johns specified.

"The same floor?" the man asked, dismayed. "I'm sorry, sir, but with the bulk of your party on that floor also, I'm afraid we might not be able to fit—"

"Mr. Robinson?" Johns said, turning to the agent.

Robinson looked pained, but said, "I'll take care of it, sir."

Apparently, he had been instructed to try to accommodate as many of Johns' demands as possible. Johns was a genius, and although he was a monumental pain in the ass as well, he was being treated like a genius.

"We'll wait in the main lounge," Johns told him.

Sherry and I accompanied him to the lounge, which was right off the main lobby. The lounge was made up of high ceilings and wood walls bathed in artificial sunlight.

"Pretty place," I commented, directing my comment to Sherry Johns. She just smiled wanly and nodded, and that was my last attempt at trying to make conversation.

Robinson came over and said, "Diamond has the room right next to yours, Doctor Johns. I hope that's satisfactory?"

We followed Robinson to the lobby and took the elevator to the eighth floor. As soon as he unlocked the door I brushed by him, saying, "Excuse me." He fumed, but remained silent.

The furnishings in the room had an old, distinctly Grecian flavor. The chairs and tables had curved legs, the beds were low to the floor and resembled divans more than beds. The Johns had a suite, and with it came a full bath and a refrigerator. Nothing in the room looked suspicious so I stuck my head out the door and said, "All clear."

Johns allowed Sherry to precede him into the room, and Robinson followed. Behind him came the men with the luggage.

"My room?" I asked Robinson.

He glared at me and said, "Next door. This is 818, you're in 816. Your bag is already there."

Robinson dismissed the other men, and then stood there looking at me.

"Diamond will be staying, Mr. Robinson," Johns said. "Anything you have to say to me, you can say in front of him."

"But sir—" the man protested.

"We can take the time to call General Davies if you like, Mr. Robinson," Johns said.

Robinson wanted to explode, but he was a pro and he showed admirable self control, under the circumstances.

"We are all here," he began to explain, "under the guise of businessman attending a shipping industry conference. The conference rooms are on the mezzanine which is between the fourth and fifth floors. Someone will be here each day to escort you there."

"When does the conference start?" I asked.

"Not until tomorrow," Robinson answered without looking at me.

"Are the others here yet?" Johns asked.

"Not yet. They should all arrive by tomorrow, though. The actual conference won't start until day after tomorrow," he corrected himself, "but we will be gathering tomorrow, just to get to know—or at least recognize—one another."

"Wonderful," Johns said, sarcastically.

"Will I be allowed to go into the conference room with Doctor Johns?" I asked.

"No," Robinson said, and he seemed to get some satisfaction out of telling me that. "Nobody goes into the conference room but the five scientists. There are two exits from that room, and we'll be covering both." He grinned a little for the first time since we'd met and said, "You could probably go and take in the sights, Diamond. Be a shame to force Mrs. Johns to sit in her room while her husband was working."

"That might not be such a bad idea, Diamond," Johns said. "We'll talk about it."

I nodded.

"We'd like to rest now," the doctor told Robinson.

"Of course. I'm in room 842. If you need anything, just give me a call." Robinson exchanged glances with me, and then left the room.

"I get the distinct impression that I'm not his favorite person," I commented as he left.

"Making friends with him is not part of your job," Johns told me. "You let me worry about him."

"Sure, Doc," I said.

"Please don't call me Doc." He was showing some irritability that I thought might have been from the trip, so I didn't reply to that.

"Are you folks going to want something to eat?" I asked.

"No," Johns said.

"Lucas, I am a bit hungry," Sherry Johns said, rather timidly.

He looked at her, still seeming irritated, and then his face softened a bit and he said, "Of course, dear, you can feel free to order from room service, or go out and eat." Johns turned to me and said, "I'll let you know if I want you to escort Mrs. Johns to dinner, Diamond."

"Excuse me, Doctor," I said, "but my job is to protect you—"

"Your job is to protect myself and *my wife*," he countered. If I stay in the room and my wife goes out, she will require your services more than I will. I think I can survive with the presence of Mr. Robinson and his men for an hour or so."

Actually, I felt that he would be quite safe with Robinson and his men on the floor, so I didn't argue.

"As you wish, Doctor," I said, "you're paying the freight."

"Yes, I am, Mr. Diamond," he said, formally. "Please, remember that."

"Oh, I will, Doctor," I assured him. "I will. I'll go to my room and wait for your call. Excuse me. Mrs. Johns?"

"Yes, of course," she replied, and I left the room.

As I was about to enter my room, that sixth sense you develop when you're in the business a long time, told me something wasn't right.

I pulled Wilhelmina out, used my key on the

door, kicked it open and went in hard and low, with my gun held straight out in front of me.

"You won't need that," Larry Robinson, the agent in charge told me. "I'd just like to know what the hell Nick Carter is doing horning in on my operation."

SEVEN

"Hello, Larry," I said, kicking the door shut and putting my gun away.

"Let's save the greetings for later, Nick. Why don't you tell me what you're doing here?"

"I'm working, same as you," I explained. He was seated on the couch in the center of the room; I sat in a padded armchair.

"Don't give me a song and a dance, Nick," Larry Robinson warned me. "I don't want to hear that you've retired, changed your name and gone private. I want it straight."

"I'll give it to you straight, Larry, don't worry," I assured him, and indeed I would have to. I knew Larry Robinson too well to try and put something over on him.

Larry and I had worked together a few times in the past, and we'd always gotten along, but he was upset—and rightfully so—at my unannounced appearance right in the middle of his operation.

I ran it down for him by the numbers and finished up by telling him, "I had no idea you were the agent in charge of this, Larry, or I would have insisted you be told."

"Yeah, okay," Larry said, running it over in his mind. "So you're not here to take over."

"Hell, no, Larry. I'm Nick Diamond, hotshot private eye from D.C. You're in charge of this show."

"Okay," Larry said. He ran his hands through his close cut black hair and then took a deep breath in an effort to relax himself.

"Would you like to run it down for me?" I asked him.

"Sure, why not. You've got to know the lay-out," he conceded. "We've got five scientists, Nick. A Russian, a German, an Englishman and a Frenchman. With Johns, that makes five."

"No Chinese?" I asked.

"They refused to come."

"I'm not surprised, but they may be missing something," I pointed out.

"Or they may feel that they're far enough ahead of us not to have to worry about it."

"I doubt it."

"I hope you're right. Anyway, each scientist has a security crew, and although only five people will actually participate in the conference, we've got a good crowd here for this thing."

"I can imagine. Who's not here, yet?" I asked.

"The Russians," he answered. "Probably want to make a grand entrance."

"I hope they're all sending representatives

who can speak English," I said.

"That's definite. It was necessary in order for us to keep down the number of people who will actually be in the room with them. No security men, no translators. Just those five men."

"No distractions," I commented.

"Except maybe Doctor Johns," Larry replied. "From what I hear, he didn't want to be here, and he's not going to make this exchange of information very easy."

"That's very true," I agreed.

"He sure has a sexy-looking wife," Larry remarked, "but doesn't she ever talk?"

"That's not what he married her for," I said, remembering her words.

"Well, I know that," he laughed, obviously misunderstanding me. "You don't do much talking to a woman who looks like that."

"That's not what I meant," I said quickly, and he gave me a funny look. "Look, Larry, she wants to go and eat, and the doctor wants me to go with her."

"He's staying in the room?"

"Right."

"Don't worry," he said, rising, "we'll have him covered."

"I know it," I answered. "I'm not worried. He's going to call me when his wife is ready to go, so I want to clean up a bit first."

"Sure, Nick. Uh, listen, I'm sorry I jumped on you, but—"

"No problem, Larry. Don't apologize."

"Okay," Larry said, putting his hand out. We shook hands and he said, "It'll be nice working with you again."

"Sure," I replied, "just don't forget my name?"

"Okay, Diamond," he said. "I'll see you later."

EIGHT

"This is superb," Sherry said, cutting another generous slice out of her meat.

We had decided to have dinner at the hotel's roof garden restaurant, where we had a spectacular view of the Tomb of the Unknown Soldier. Sherry seemed overwhelmed by the menu which was extensive and quite diverse, so I took the liberty of ordering a traditional lamb dish for both of us.

"I'm glad you like it." I had also ordered ouzo and poured her a glass. When she tasted it, her eyes lit up.

"*Whoo*, strong," she said, and then took another sip adding, "but good."

I picked up my glass, "*Steenee yamas!*" I toasted.

"What does that mean?" she asked, smiling.

"Good health to us."

She smiled even wider, "*Steenee yamas!*"

The changing of the guard at the Tomb of the Unknown Soldier takes place every hour, twenty minutes before the hour. When it was time, Sherry watched intently, enjoying the pomp and circumstance of the occasion. We could just about hear the regimental band from where we were as the sound carried through the evening.

"It was beautiful," she said, turning back to her food. "What was this called again?"

"*Arni yiouvetsi,*" I answered. "Lamb in tomato sauce."

"It's really delicious. What did you get?"

"*Yuvetsi,* lamb with noodles. Would you like to taste?"

She hesitated, then said, "Please."

I speared some and extended my fork. She opened her mouth and gently took the food from the fork. I found myself watching her full lips the whole time.

"*Mmm,*" she said, "it's good, but mine is more tasty. I think I'll have just a little more ouzo."

I smiled and poured her a little more, which she drank in sips. When she was finished I told the waiter to bring us coffee, and he cleared the table. With the coffee he brought the check.

"I'll see that you get that back," Sherry said when she saw me examining the bill.

"Oh no," I protested. "This dinner is on me."

"Thank you, Nick," she smiled. "Thanks for being so nice, so easy to talk to."

"The way I see it," I told her, "you need someone to talk to."

She looked away at that, staring at the Unknown Soldier again.

"I guess I'm also easy not to talk to," I said, digging in my pocket for some money.

"Nick, I'm sorry—"

"Forget it," I said, counting out the right amount. "Do you want to go for a walk before going back?"

"Oh, yes."

We were only about a block from Syntagma, or Constitution Square. From there it was a short walk to the Plaka, probably the liveliest part of Athens.

"When the conference starts," I said, "and your husband is behind closed doors for a few hours, I'll take you out again. You can do some shopping and we can have lunch in a taverna."

"That'll be lovely," she said.

"We'd better get back."

About a block from the hotel I stopped, pulling her into a doorway. "What's going on, Sherry? What's with you and Johns? Do you love the guy, or what?"

"Nick, don't—" she said, turning her head away, but I grabbed her by the shoulders and made her face me.

"What's wrong with him?" I asked, letting her shoulders go. "Not only does he never talk to you, he never touches you. If I was married to you, I wouldn't be able to keep my hands off of you."

She stared into my face then and said, "If only you were married to me, Nick."

She was so close I could feel her breath on my face. I put my arms around her, pulled her closer and kissed her. Her mouth was hot beneath mine, willing.

"Nick—" she started to say, pulling her mouth

away, and that's when they hit us.

There were three of them; when one of the trio grabbed for Sherry I didn't waste any time. I flicked my wrist and Hugo jumped into my hand. I slashed her assailant's face, and he fell back. A second man moved in and threw a punch which glanced off my shoulder. I kicked out and caught him on the knee, driving him back as well.

I told Sherry to stay inside the doorway, but I moved out. The man I'd slashed was on one knee, trying to keep his face from falling off. The other two came back at me, but they didn't know how to approach the knife. They weren't pros, and for that reason I left Wilhelmina where she was, safe and snug beneath my left arm.

"Come on," I said to them, not knowing whether they could understand me or not. They were both watching the knife, so I stepped in and struck with my left hand while they watched Hugo in my right.

I hit the gimpy one flush on the face with my left fist and he fell backward. The other one had the presence of mind to throw a kick at me. I turned and took it on my thigh, but I felt the shock of it down my leg.

He was in close at that point and I could have driven Hugo right through his sternum, but I didn't want to kill him. I reached out and took off a small piece of his chin, and he clasped his hands to his face and howled. It was the gimpy one who shouted something to the other two, and they all took off down the street.

Sherry stepped out of the doorway. "What was happening there? What did they want?"

"Money, I suppose," I said. I slipped Hugo back into place and then started rubbing my thigh, trying to work the numbness out. The man who had kicked me had been wearing some kind of a heavy work boot.

"Are you all right?" she asked.

"Yes, I'm fine," I said, flexing the leg, staring in the direction of the fleeing men. I had a funny idea rolling around inside of my head, but no time to examine it at the moment.

I put weight on the leg and found that it was working perfectly. I took Sherry by the elbow and she looked up into my face.

"Shall we continue our conversation?" I asked.

"I—I don't think so," she stammered.

"I didn't think so, either," I said. "Come on, I'll take you back and you can tell your husband about the excitement he missed."

NINE

"What do you think they were after if it wasn't money?" Larry Robinson asked.

After dropping Sherry Johns off at her room, and not waiting to talk to the doctor, I had gone back to my room and phoned Robinson. When he came over I recounted what had happened on the street.

"If you stalked a man and a woman to take their money, who would you grab?" I asked.

"I'm old fashioned," he said. "I'd assume that the man had the money and grab him."

"Well, they grabbed for her first, not me. I think they would have pulled her away from me, and then two of them would have fought me while the other took off with her."

He stared at me and asked, "You think they were trying to snatch her?"

"I do."

"But why?"

"What's the next best thing to snatching the doctor?" I asked.

"Snatching her," he said. "Right. Then they could get him to come to them. Did you tell this to the doctor and his wife?"

"No."

"Why not?"

"I didn't want to worry them."

"Oh, I see. You going to let them go on thinking it was just a mugging attempt?"

"I'll let them think what they like, but I think we'd—you'd better have a couple of men watching her."

"When she's not with you, you mean?" he asked.

I looked at him, but he didn't seem to mean anything by the remark other than what it said. "Yes, that's right. While he's in conference with the others, he'll be yours, she'll be mine."

"Okay. What are you going to do now?" he asked, getting up and preparing to leave.

"I'm going to get some sleep," I said.

"Yeah, I could use some sleep, too."

He started for the door and I called out, "Larry."

"Yeah?"

"Have you bugged their room?"

"Well," he said, spreading his hands, "we have to be able to keep tabs on what goes on, just in case."

"I just wanted to know," I explained.

"Sure. I'll see you in the morning."

"Okay, and make sure you keep acting like you don't like me," I suggested. "We don't want the doctor suddenly wondering why we've become friends overnight."

"Good point, Shamus," he said. "See you tomorrow."

"Right."

After he left I took a shower, allowing the hot water to soak into my bruised thigh. Sliding into bed with Wilhelmina nearby, I thought about the three men who had attacked us—who had put them up to it?

Was one of the other governments already trying to sabotage the meetings? And if so, why used unskilled labor—and Greeks at that. When the guy whose chin I'd cut called out to the other two, it had been in Greek.

And what about those shoes? The one who had kicked me had been wearing heavy work shoes, and I was fairly certain that the others had been, also.

What did that mean, if anything?

It meant that I was going to have to keep a damn good eye on Sherry Johns for the duration of this meeting.

TEN

I got to show Sherry Johns a little bit of Greece earlier than I'd expected. Johns called me the next morning and asked me to come to his room. First he went over the incident with the three men—briefly—and then he told me his plans for the day.

"Diamond, I want to thank you for protecting my wife last night, from those muggers. I'm going to include a bonus for you. Sherry was very frightened and she—we'd like to show our appreciation."

"There's no need to thank me for doing my job."

He nodded, turned to his wife and said, "You see? The man is a professional. I told you that."

She nodded to him and looked at me as if I were crazy to have talked myself out of a bonus.

"All right, Diamond. My day calls for me to be in my room, working," he said, getting to business.

"What about tonight?"

"Oh, I'll be at their little gathering tonight, but

I've got work to do, work I should be in Washington doing," he said, in disgust. "I can't allow this farce to interfere with my work. Now my wife agrees with me on this, Diamond, so she has also agreed to go out and see Greece with you instead of me."

"Doctor—" I started, but he went right on through me.

"In light of what happened last night, I would feel much better if she was with you," he said.

"Doctor, my main function is to—"

"Mr. Diamond," he said, showing impatience, "if I stay in my room all the time, just how much danger can I be in? All of the security men from those other countries are also on this floor, protecting their people. I am amply protected right here."

"But your wife—"

"My wife would like some breakfast, Diamond. I'd appreciate it if you would take her. You can also let that security man, Robinson, know that I'll be in my room for most of the day." He turned to Sherry and said, "Go with Diamond, dear. See Greece, do as much sightseeing as you like. Stay out for lunch, too." He turned back to me and said, "Just be back in time for us to get ready for that cozy get acquainted session this evening. All right?"

"Whatever you say, Doctor Johns."

"That's right," he replied. "Now go on, I have a lot of work to do and I would like to get started."

"I'll get my things," Sherry said. She went and got her purse and a light jacket, came back and said, "I'm ready."

Johns was already seated at a table with a bunch of papers spread out in front of him.

"Have a nice day, dear," he said without looking up.

She stood there staring at him, as if waiting for him to look up, and finally she just looked at me and headed for the door.

We didn't speak in the hall and I told her to wait at the elevator while I talked to Robinson.

When Robinson opened the door to his room and saw me he asked, "What's up?"

Before he could mention my real name or even sound like we were old friends, I stepped aside a little so he could see Sherry standing down the hall. She was close enough to hear everything that was said.

"What do you want, Diamond?" he growled.

"I just wanted to let you know that I'm taking Mrs. Johns out for breakfast and some sightseeing. We'll probably be out for lunch as well. Doctor Johns will be in his room all day until we return."

"Just make sure you get back in time for the first meeting, tonight," he said. "I'm sure the Doctor will want his wife to attend with him."

I said, "Don't worry," and winked at him. He slammed the door in my face.

"He doesn't like you very much, does he?" she asked in the elevator.

"He doesn't think I'm necessary," I told her.

"He takes it personally that your husband would hire his own bodyguard."

"I see."

Before we reached the main floor I asked, "Are we going to be awkward all day?"

She looked at me and then she smiled and said, "I'm sorry," as if scolding herself.

"Look, let's not be awkward, and let's not be sorry, okay? Let's see if we can't get you to enjoy being in Greece a little bit."

She smiled again, a wide one this time, and said, "Okay, Nick."

"Why don't we have breakfast in the Syntagma? There are plenty of shops and restaurants. We can eat and then do some shopping or sightseeing, whichever you like."

"Can we do both?" she asked, smiling like a mischievous little girl.

We had breakfast in a little coffee shop and I found that Sherry Johns had as much of an appetite in the morning as she did in the evening. We both had eggs, sausages, potatoes, toast, coffee and juice—a very American breakfast.

"I'd like to ask you something," she said as our meals were set in front of us.

"Okay, go ahead," I said.

"About last night—those men, I mean."

"What about them?"

"Well, you wear a gun, don't you?" she asked.

"I do."

"Why didn't you just shoot them, instead of using the knife?"

I smiled patiently and said, "There was no need to shoot them. In fact, if you hadn't been there, I wouldn't have even used the knife."

"Why not?"

I shoveled some eggs onto a piece of toast and hesitated to explain. "They weren't professional, Sherry. My only concern was taking care of them without you getting hurt. If you weren't there, I could have done that without a knife."

"Could you have killed them?"

I frowned at her, wondering what she was after. Some kind of vicarious thrill? "I could have, Sherry, yes. Why are you asking?"

"I watched you the whole time," she said. "You knew what you were doing at every moment. I think that takes a special kind of man. I think maybe you're a very dangerous man, Nick Diamond."

"Sometimes," I replied, "but not at breakfast."

"No," she agreed, "but in dark doorways . . ."

"Ah, good," I said, "we're not feeling awkward anymore."

"Well, why should we?" she asked, leaning forward and gazing at me over our breakfast. "It was only a kiss."

"That's true," I said. "It was only a kiss."

The rest of the day went very easily between us. Our first stop was a bank, where we exchanged some currency. The main denomination is the drachma, forty-two of which are equal to one American dollar. I've always admired the Greek ingenuity of making their paper currency easily recognizable—the fifty drachma note is blue; the one hundred, red; the five hundred, green; the one thousand, brown.

After a brief visit to the National Archaeological Museum, we headed for the House of Parliament. The Parliament building used to be the Royal Palace. It's a large, squarish yellow building with a marble forecourt that faces Constitution Square. King Otto, who was put on the throne after the war with Turkey, used a very interesting method to choose the site for this building. He hung meat in different parts of town, and erected the building where the maggots were the slowest to gather. We also got a closer look at the Changing of the Guard at the Tomb of the Unknown Soldier.

We hit the Acropolis just before lunch which, in Greece, never starts before two p.m. It has to do with Athenian office hours. Most people start working at about eight a.m., work nonstop until about one or two in the afternoon, break for lunch and a siesta until five, and then go back to work until eight or eight-thirty p.m. Dinner never starts before nine p.m.

Acropolis means "upper city." It's built on a rock 515 feet above sea level. The Acropolis contains four ancient buildings, and one modern one which is the Acropolis Museum. The Parthenon, the most famous of the ancient buildings, was built between 447 and 432 B.C., the time of Pericles, and was dedicated to the virgin goddess Athena.

"That's the most beautiful thing I've ever

seen," Sherry said as we trudged back down the hill to the city.

"It's impressive, all right," I agreed.

We had lunch in a taverna and paid an exorbitant amount of money for it, which reminded her of something.

"Why didn't you accept the bonus Lucas wanted to give you?" she asked.

"Because he didn't want to give it to me," I replied.

"All right, so I talked him into it. You still should have accepted it. Look at what you've spent between last night and today. Look at this bill—" she started to say, reaching for it, but I got to it first.

"I will," I promised, putting it down at my elbow, "soon enough."

"You'll tell Lucas you want the bonus when we get back?"

"No."

"Why not?"

"Because I want you to know that I took you to dinner, shopping, sightseeing and to lunch because I wanted to, and not because he told me to. Is that a good enough answer for you?"

It was. She looked down at her hands, then started gathering up her packages, saying, "I'll carry some of these back to the hotel. We'd better get back."

I called the waiter over and left a generous tip for him and the *miero,* or busboy. They had both been very attentive during the meal.

When Sherry opened the door to her room, while one of Robinson's men watched from down the hall, and we entered, Johns was exactly where we had left him. The only change was a pot of coffee and a dirty cup.

"Lucas," she called out.

His head jerked up and he looked surprised.

"Back already?" he asked, frowning at his watch.

"It's late, Lucas," she said. "Almost four-thirty."

"That's not late," he argued. "I've still got time before we have to go downstairs. Would you call room service for more coffee, dear?" he asked her.

"Of course," she said. She turned to me as I put the packages down and all the animation that had been in her face throughout the day was gone. "Thank you, Mr. Diamond, for a wonderful day."

"It was my pleasure, Mrs. Johns," I answered. To Johns I said, "I'll be by to pick you both up at seven, Doctor."

He mumbled something and didn't look up.

"We'll be ready," Sherry said. She took my arm and walked to the door with me. She mouthed "Thank you" and squeezed my arm. I stepped out into the hall and she closed the door gently behind me. When I turned to walk down to my room I saw Larry Robinson looking out his door and waved at him. He moved back inside and shut his door.

I went into my room and ran the day through

my mind. We'd done enough walking to pick up a tail if there was one, and I hadn't spotted anyone following us. Apparently, whoever had planned the attempt to grab Sherry the night before chose not to come right back the next day with another. That is, of course, assuming that last night had not simply been a mugging attempt, which was the assumption I was going on.

The rest of the day and evening should be safe enough, I figured, what with all of the security people who would be around, but I still intended to stay close to Sherry until the introductory session was over.

And maybe even after, too.

ELEVEN

Two rooms had been set aside by the hotel for our "convention." One was a large lounge with a bar; the other was the main meeting room, where only the five scientists would be allowed.

On that first evening we would use only the lounge. The sole purpose of this gathering was for the five scientists to meet and identify each other.

"This should be stimulating," Johns said, sarcastically as we entered.

"Lucas . . ." Sherry said.

"I know, dear, I know," he said.

"Doctor, please don't go anywhere without one of my men or myself next to you," Robinson told him.

"Or Diamond," Johns said.

"All right," Robinson said, sounding properly disgusted, "or your man." He turned to Sherry and said, "Mrs. Johns, I'd appreciate it if you would abide by the same rule?"

"Of course."

"Let's go mingle, then," he said, and we moved into the room.

"Diamond, would you get my wife a brandy?" Johns said.

"Of course," I replied, "and anything for you, Doctor?"

"A ginger ale, I think."

I went to the bar and Larry Robinson came along.

"Look at him," he said, looking at Johns, "he's standing there like he's the Pope or something and all the rest of them should come over and kiss his ring."

"I'm going to bring them their drinks," I told him, "and then I'm coming back for one for myself. You want to point the others out to me then?"

"Sure. Hurry back." He turned to the bar to order himself a drink and I carried the drink I had in each hand to Doctor and Mrs. Johns.

"Thank you," Sherry said, taking her drink. She looked lovely in a low cut black dress that left one rounded shoulder bare. That shoulder made you want to lean right over and plant a kiss on it, but I resisted and handed Doctor Johns his ginger ale. He took it without a thank you and continued to survey all that he thought he was superior to.

"Are you going to talk to some of these other scientists?" I asked him.

He looked at me and said, "Only when I have to, Diamond, only when I absolutely have to."

I went back to the bar and ordered a bourbon. When I had it firmly gripped in my hand, I turned around and said to Robinson, "Start pointing."

"Let me find them first," he said, and then, "Okay, got one. See that tall drink of water over there against the wall."

The man he was pointing to had a ramrod straight stance and stood at least six-four. He had slicked down black hair, a black moustache and he was wearing a tuxedo.

"Is he Russian?"

"Yes. His name's Boris Ravinsky. He's fifty-three, and he dyes his hair and his moustache. Thinks he's a ladies' man."

"What does the lady next to him think?" I asked.

The lady next to him was a handsome woman who appeared to be in her early forties, with a striking gray streak that ran through the middle of her coal black hair.

"That's his girl friend, Natasha. His wife is back home with the kids. Now look over there, by the window. The portly one. That's Henri Bouchet. He's not more than a year or two older than Johns, but he looks a hell of a lot older."

Bouchet had thinning dark hair on his head, a pencil-thin moustache and cheeks that looked like they might be full of food.

Robinson continued to look around the room and the next scientist he pointed out was Doctor Klaus Kruger, from Germany. Kruger looked like he was about four foot ten, with a huge bulbous nose, and tiny eyes and mouth. He was holding what looked like a glass of milk.

"I was beginning to get nervous that Doctor

Johns would get suspicious if I spent any more time with Robinson.

"Who's the fifth one?" I asked.

"She's not here yet," he said.

"She?"

"She," he said, pushing away from the bar, "and you won't need my help to pick her out. Not if I know you."

"Wait a minute—"

"I got work to do, pal," he said. I watched as he walked over to stand with the Johns, freeing one of his men to get himself a drink.

I kept switching my eyes among the other three scientists who were present, and they had had a minimum of two security people standing with them at all times. They had to have others floating around, though, and to round out the number of people in there, there had to be some hotel security people as well.

Suddenly, everyone in the room seemed to turn toward the entrance. The woman standing in the doorway was breathtaking with shoulder-length auburn hair, green eyes and a wide, full-lipped mouth: the fifth scientist.

About five six, she had full, ripe breasts that couldn't be hidden by the severe cut of the suit she was wearing. Her skirt covered her knees, but her calves were shapely and firm.

She was flanked by four security men, and what appeared to be one security woman who was quite homely by comparison. She made a slow survey of the room before heading in my direction.

"Hello," she said, stopping right in front of me.

"Hi."

"Would you like to buy me a drink?" she asked.

"The bar is complimentary," I pointed out. "What will you have?"

"Scotch."

I turned to face the bar and she moved close enough so that I could smell her hair. One of her security men crowded in on my other side.

"Does he think I'm going to poison your scotch?" I asked her.

"I can't get rid of them," she said, sounding apologetic. "I'm sorry, but they think I'm important."

I handed her the drink and said, "So, you're the lady scientist?"

"Couldn't I be important if I wasn't?"

"Without a doubt."

"Then what does it matter?" she asked.

"I just like to know who I'm talking to," I said.

"Very well, then," she said, raising her glass. "My name is Diana Ridgeway and I'm the British representative at this gathering of the great minds. And you?"

"My name is Nick Diamond. I'm here with Doctor Lucas Johns, from America."

"Oh yes, the genius who thought he was too good to come here and meet the rest of us," she said. "What are you, his assistant?"

"Nope. I'm his personal bodyguard. Uh, who's the woman with you?"

"She's my aunt," she answered, with a twinkle in her eyes, "and she's sort of a good luck charm. I don't go anywhere without her." She smiled widely, showing me incredibly straight, white teeth, and said, "You know, this meeting may not be as boring as I thought it would be."

"Not if you have anything to say about it," I agreed.

She held her drink up to her mouth, stuck her tongue in it, ran it around her lips and then said, "See you later, Mr. Diamond."

"Nick," I said.

"Him, too," she said, and then she turned and walked away.

I took a deep breath, watched her walk off with her security people and then looked over to where the Johns were standing and found Sherry Johns watching me. There was no expression on her face, but I knew she'd been watching Diana and me, and I didn't know how to react to that. I turned away and ordered another bourbon.

"There was smoke coming out of that lady's ears, Nick," Larry Robinson said, coming up alongside me and ordering another drink.

"Whose ears?" I asked.

"Mrs. Johns. She saw you talking to Diana Ridgeway, and she didn't seem to like how close together you two were standing."

"There's nothing going on there between Mrs. Johns and me, Larry. Don't start."

"I'm not starting, Nick. If there's nothing going on, it's not because that lady doesn't want there to be. Take my word for it."

"Okay, Larry, I'll take your word for it. Just drop it, okay?"

"Okay," he said, accepting his fresh drink from the bartender, "but be careful, huh? We got enough explosive situations here without adding one more."

"Yeah."

I turned to watch him return to the Johns and saw that one of the other representatives had finally chosen to approach Doctor Lucas Johns. He wasn't talking to her though.

Sherry Johns was the one who was talking to Diana Ridgeway.

TWELVE

There were sparks passing between the two lovely women, but no violence erupted, and eventually Diana Ridgeway continued on, speaking to all of the other representatives in turn.

Doctor Lucas Johns, on the other hand, never moved from that corner, and none of the other representatives chose to approach him, which probably suited him just fine.

When Diana Ridgeway left the Johns I walked over with my fresh drink and asked, "Can I get anyone a refill?"

"No, thank you, Diamond," Johns said. He was answering for both of them without even asking Sherry, first.

"Mrs. Johns?" I asked.

"I don't think so," she said. She turned to her husband and said, "Darling, I have a terrible headache. I'm going back to the room to lie down."

He looked at her and said, "All right, dear." He turned to me and said, "Diamond, take Mrs. Johns upstairs and stay with her until I return. I'm quite safe here with these gentlemen."

"Doctor—"

"Diamond!" he said, and we stared at each other for a few moments until I felt Sherry's hand on my elbow. It was done so that no one else could see it, but her insistent pressure was unmistakable.

"Very well, Doctor," I finally conceded. "As you wish."

"Thank you, Diamond," he said. "Thank you very much."

He was getting to the point where he was perfecting the art of sarcasm—and it was starting to get harder for me to ignore.

I took Sherry's elbow and said, "Mrs. Johns?"

"I'll see you upstairs, Lucas," she said to the doctor.

"I might be a few hours," he said. "Don't wait up for me."

She nodded to Larry Robinson and his men and Larry offered, "I could send one of my men along, also, Doctor."

Sherry seemed about to object, but the doctor got there first. "I think Mr. Diamond has proven he can amply protect my wife, Mr. Robinson. You know about the mugging incident, of course."

"Of course."

"Then I'm sure you agree, no matter what you may think of Mr. Diamond, personally."

"I have no opinions about Mr. Diamond, personally," Larry told Johns.

"Then it's settled. I will see you later, my

dear," he said to Sherry, and we were on our way.

In the elevator I braved the definite chill that was in the air and said, "I'm sorry you're not feeling well."

"You seemed to be having a good time," she said in clipped tones.

"I was becoming acquainted with the other representatives."

"Yes, I noticed that, too. Very acquainted!"

I let it drop when the elevator doors opened and we walked to her room.

"Will you be all right?" I asked her.

"I'll be just fine," she replied, fitting her key in the lock and turning it viciously.

"If you need anything—"

"Good night," she said. She stepped into her room and closed the door firmly behind her.

I went back to my room, determined not to let her mood bother me. I had taken off my shirt and tie when there was a knock at the door. I answered without putting anything on.

It was Sherry Johns.

"Nick, I—" she started, and then stopped when she realized I was bare to the waist. She seemed to be studying my chest and shoulders, and it could have been embarrassing if anyone came along and saw us that way.

"Sherry—" I began, but her actions interrupted me.

She put both of her hands against my chest and pushed me back into the room. Then she stepped into the room and closed the door behind her.

Once she was in the room with me I became aware that she was wearing a robe, and that she apparently had nothing on underneath. Her nipples were very well defined and made little turrets against the material of her robe.

"Look, Sherry, you shouldn't be—"

"I want you, Nick," she said. She stepped closer and started to run her hands over my shoulders and chest. "I think I've wanted you from the first moment you walked in Lucas' office and I saw you."

I started to speak again but she prevented it by kissing me, hard. She forced her tongue between my lips and it roamed around my mouth eagerly. My hands went around her and cupped the cheeks of her behind, and I didn't seem to have any control over them. I could feel the heat of her flesh right through the robe. Her breasts were mashed against my chest and I could feel the hard little nubs of her nipples.

"Sherry," I said breathlessly when she removed her mouth, "we don't have time."

She stepped away from me a couple of feet and said, "We'll make time."

She unbelted her robe, removed it from her shoulder and shrugged it to the floor. Her body was flawless, the skin pale and smooth. Her breasts were full, and the nipples were brown, with wide areolas.

"I know you want me, Nick," she said. "You haven't made any secret about it. And I don't think it's because of the way I look. I think it's because of the way I am.". She came up to me again and pushed her naked breasts against my chest. Her hands went down to my pants and started to undo them. "No one's ever wanted me like that before, Nick. No one."

I ran my hands lightly over her back and she shivered against me. We kissed again and our tongues wrestled back and forth. When she had my pants loosened she pulled them down and I stepped out of them. I had already taken my shoes and socks off, so all she had to do was remove my briefs to make me accessible to her mouth. She was so intent on working on me that she didn't notice when I reached down and very carefully removed Pierre from my thigh.

She brought me to incredible readiness with her mouth and tongue and I drew her to her feet to kiss her again. I picked her up, carried her to the bed and placed her on it gently.

"Are you sure?" I asked.

"Oh," she replied, "I'm very sure, Nick."

I lay down next to her and kissed her mouth gently, then her neck, and then started nibbling on her nipples. She caught her breath and took my head gently in her hands, just holding it there. When I began to suck on her nipples she started to moan and run her fingers through my hair.

"Oh, yes, Nick," she said, "it's been so long . . ."

As I continued to work on her breasts with my mouth I slipped my hand between her legs and found her wet and ready. I inserted first one finger, and then two, and she lifted her hips off the bed to meet them.

"Oh, God . . ." she cried out as I worked her in both areas, "Oh, yes!"

I abandoned her nipples and began to kiss her belly, and then worked my way lower until I was able to replace my fingers with my tongue. As I inserted my tongue into her, I used my finger to stimulate her clitoris and she began to writhe and buck beneath me. Finally, I reached up and took her stiff little nub into my mouth and used my teeth and tongue to bring her to an orgasm.

She cried out, gripping my head tightly and tossing her head from side to side as she rode out the waves of pleasure that were racking her senses.

When her orgasm receded, she said, "Oh, Nick, I can't wait anymore. Please, make it now . . ."

I teased her a bit by working my way back up her body with my mouth, pausing at her nipples to once again suck them ardently. My erection became imprisoned between her thighs and she began to roll it by moving her legs.

"All right," I told her, against her mouth, "all right . . ."

I raised myself above her and when I poked against the entrance to her vagina she opened her legs as wide as she could and I slid in with no friction at all.

"Oh, God . . ." she said again, but she drew it out into what sounded like a great sigh of relief.

Slowly we sought a rhythm that suited both of us, and when we found it, it was as if we had joined together and become one person.

"Oh, yes, Nick. I knew it, I knew it would be like this for us . . ."

I kissed her and continued to take her in long, slow strokes. She moaned into my mouth and encircled me with her arms and her legs. I was enjoying her like I hadn't enjoyed another woman for a long time. I was enjoying the feel of her, the taste, the smell, everything about her, and I knew she felt the same way.

As our tempo began to increase her moans became louder and louder until they were almost screams. In the back of my mind I could see Johns coming back to the room, not finding her there, and then hearing her through the walls.

Would he care?

I felt a rush building up in my legs and loins and did my best to quell it. I didn't want this to end yet. I prolonged it for as long as I could, but finally the tempo got to the point where it was physically impossible. It was as if someone had popped a cork on a bottle of champagne that had been previously shaken up, and I emptied myself inside of her with incredible force.

THIRTEEN

"I guess I married him because he was the only man who didn't want to take me to bed the minute he saw me," she said. "I got tired of working the chorus lines and hearing promises of better things if only I would do the right thing, you know?"

"I can guess," I answered.

"We've been married three years, Nick, and he's never touched me. We don't even sleep in the same bed."

"Do you mean that this was the first time for you in three years?" I asked.

She gave me a look of pure chagrin and said, "Well, not exactly. Actually, the first five or six months it was actually refreshing not to have to worry about getting grabbed or pinched, but after that, I started to approach Lucas about it from time to time, but he was never interested in anything but his work."

"So why did he marry you?"

"I guess he's the only one who knows that.

Maybe he just figured it would help with whatever social functions he had to attend."

"Has he ever asked you to be . . . nice to anyone at any of these functions?"

"Never," she said with a very positive nod of her head. "Anyway, after that, every so often I would . . . meet somebody, you know?"

Could I blame her? Then again, how did I feel about being one of those "somebodies."

She raised herself up in bed on one elbow and touched my mouth with her other hand. "Don't be upset. I only did that a few times, I swear, and never with the same man."

I frowned and said, "I don't know if that's better or worse."

She leaned down and kissed me on the mouth with those wonderfully soft lips and said, "I don't know if I can explain."

"I don't know if you really have to, Sherry," I said. "I'm not complaining."

"But if you are thinking that way, then I do. Nick, you're a special man. I knew that even before I decided to do this."

"And when did you decide?"

"Downstairs," she said, "when I saw Diana Ridgeway making a big play for you. I thought, if I didn't do this now, you and she might . . ."

"Sherry, what's going to happen when your husband gets back to your room?"

"I'll be there," she said. "I haven't been here that long, and I'm sure he's not back yet. I'll go now," she added, and got up. I watched as she put her robe back on, and then drove her hands deep into the pockets.

"Nick, don't think badly of me, please."

"I don't, Sherry, believe me," I said, truthfully.

"If I did anything wrong, it was marrying Lucas in the first place."

"You could fix that, you know."

She laughed without humor. "And do what, Nick? Go back to the chorus lines?" She walked to the bed, leaned over and kissed me warmly, with her fingertips on my cheek.

"Thank you for tonight," she whispered.

I took her hand and said, "There'll be other nights, Sherry."

She smiled, touched my mouth with her fingers and left.

When she was gone I lay in bed and thought about what she'd said. Could I really blame a lovely, vital young woman whose husband never touched her for seeking satisfaction somewhere else? And was I a fool for believing her when she said that the time we'd just spent together meant more to her than that?

No, I didn't think I was a fool, and maybe I was a fool for thinking that. Time would tell.

When I couldn't sleep I called room service and asked them to send up a bottle of bourbon and some ice. When it came I sat in a chair and started to work on it.

I guess I liked Sherry Johns a lot and felt sorry for her, and the whole thing depressed me. It would be a shame for her to stay stuck in a marriage simply because she didn't think she could do anything else.

Maybe somebody had to show her what else she could do.

I was still in that chair an hour later and heard Doctor Johns, Larry Robinson and his other men get off the elevator. I heard Robinson bid Johns good night, and the doctor mumble something in return. Then I heard the door to the room next door open and close. I almost got up and walked to the wall to put my ear against it and see what I could hear, but I decided that wasn't the thing to do. The thing to do was go to bed before I got drunk.

FOURTEEN

Doctor and Mrs. Johns had breakfast in their room the next morning. I had breakfast in the hotel dining room with Larry Robinson.

"Don't worry about it," he advised me. "We can always say we were ironing out security measures."

I finally agreed, especially when he said that Uncle Sam would pick up the tab.

"That English lady doctor sure was looking you up and down last night," he observed over his eggs benedict. "She was looking for you after you left. I'm surprised she didn't show up at your room last night."

Not as surprised as she would have been if she had, I thought, but I didn't say anything.

"Did you meet any of the other security people last night?" I asked him.

"Yes, I did. The Britishers are a stiff-upper-lip bunch. Four of them and they all want to be boss. The best of the lot seems to be a gentleman named John Mount.

"The German's got three men with him. The boss is a guy named Colonel Fritz von Klemperer. The Russians, they've got two men flanking their guy. Top man's name is Mikel Destrovitch. Heard of him?"

"I have. He's one of their best men."

"Crossed his path?"

"Luckily, no. I'd hate to have to go through this whole meeting trying to duck him."

"Yeah. Anyway, the French have two men on Doctor Bouchet. Head man is Georges DuPrée, a little slip of a guy with big ideas."

"Like what?"

"He thinks we should all be working together to guard all five representatives than working alone to cover our own man—or lady, as the case may be."

"Might be a good idea? You think the rest of them would go for it?"

"I don't think we'd have any trouble convincing the English, but the Russians and the Germans?" He shook his head to indicate his opinion of their willingness to work together.

"Maybe you should propose it and see what they say, Larry. It couldn't hurt."

"You might be right," he said, rubbing his jaw and thinking it over.

"Larry, I'm going to ask you a question."

"Okay."

"I'd like you to answer it without asking any of your own," I added.

He hesitated, then said, "If it's reasonable."

"After you brought Johns back to his room last night, did you pick up anything on the bug?"

"Like—" he started to ask, then stopped and started again. "Not a peep, Nick. The Mrs. must have been asleep, and the Doctor just sacked out himself. Oh, I did hear some paper rustling, so maybe he did some work before he went to bed himself."

"Okay," I said. "Thanks."

"Sure," he said, looking puzzled. "Don't mention it."

"Did the doctor tell you his schedule?" I asked.

"No, you?"

I shook my head. "He told me to go get myself some breakfast and then come back."

"He'll probably give you his wife to take on a sightseeing tour again. You didn't seem to mind all that much yesterday."

I looked at him sharply, then relaxed and said, "You're probably right."

"You know, it's a shame that woman didn't marry someone who would treat her the way she deserved to be treated," Larry said.

"I couldn't agree with you more," I said. I finished my coffee and stood up, saying, "I'd better go up and see what my lord and master wants me to do today."

When I knocked on the Doctor's door Sherry answered.

"Good morning," she said, smiling. The smile made me think that I wouldn't find Johns in, and that turned out to be just the case.

"Where's your husband?" I asked.

She looked surprised. "He said he was going to go down to the lobby to meet you," she said. Then she looked alarmed. "Oh, no, don't tell me he—"

"He did," I said. He'd chosen to be even more difficult than he had been so far, and had skipped out without me or Robinson. Our only chance was that one of Larry's men spotted him and went after him.

"I want to use your phone," I said, walking past her.

I dialed the front desk and asked them to page Larry Robinson. When Larry came on I said, "Did you see Johns in the last few minutes?"

"Since you left? No, why?"

"He's flown the coop, Larry."

"Goddamnit!" he snapped.

"I'm going down the hall to see if any of your men went after him. Why don't you check with the hotel staff down there. I'll meet you in a few minutes."

"Okay."

I hung up and turned to Sherry. "Have you got any idea where he might have gone?"

"No. He didn't give me any indication that he was going to do anything like this."

"Shit! What's wrong with that man, anyway?"

"He doesn't like to be confined. He resents having to do what the government tells him just because they're funding him."

"I think they're doing a little more than funding him, Sherry. They've got dibs on whatever he comes up with, don't they?"

She shrugged. "I guess so. I don't get involved with his business."

"What's he working on now, Sherry? What's this meeting all about?"

"I don't have any idea, Nick, honest."

I believed her. Johns would never let her get *that* close to him.

"Sherry, do you think that Lucas Johns would, uh, sell any of his work to a foreign government?"

"You mean, would he turn traitor to his country?" she asked, looking shocked.

"I don't know why you look so surprised," I said. "He doesn't exactly strike me as the patriotic type."

"He's not after a lot of money either, Nick," she said. "He just wants to be left alone to do his work. No, I don't think Lucas is selling out his country right now. I just think he's trying to be difficult, scare Robinson and Uncle Sam a little. He'll be back."

"I hope so, but then, it might not be so bad for you if he didn't come back, would it?" I asked.

"Don't say that," she said, hugging her arms as if she were chilled.

"I'm not wishing him any harm," I told her. "I just think you'd be better off without him."

"Doing what?" she asked.

"Find somebody else," I suggested.

"And until then, do what?" she asked. "I can't go back to the line, Nick."

"There are other things you can do," I reasoned.

"Name one," she said, then she gazed at me and said, "Hey, you wouldn't need a partner, would you? Or a secretary who couldn't type or take shorthand?"

Right then and there I wished I was a two-bit private eye with an office of my own so I could give her a job.

"I wish I could, honey," I said.

Her face fell and she said, "Ah, forget it, Nick. I'll stay where I am and live with it."

"You shouldn't have to—"

She put her fingers on my lips and said, "Why don't you go out and see if you can find him before he gets himself into trouble, huh?"

I kissed her fingers and told her that I would, but I told myself that we'd talk about this again, later.

"He's done things like this too many times before for me to really worry, Nick . . . but you be careful, okay?"

"I will," I promised.

I left before she could say anything else, something that might embarrass her if Robinson or someone else listened to the tape.

I walked down the hall to Robinson's room and knocked on the door. One of his men answered, a middle-aged guy named Lynch.

"Yeah?" he asked.

"I just thought you'd like to know that Doctor Johns is gone. He's flown the coop."

"What?" he asked, looking dismayed.

"Did any of your men pick him up when he left?" I asked.

"Not that I know of, unless somebody spotted him in the lobby."

"Well, I'm going down to see what Robinson's come up with. I'd advise you to have a pretty damn good explanation for him about how the guy got off this floor without one of you going with him."

"I—" he started, but I didn't give him time to get anywhere. I turned and headed for the elevator. I was hoping that Larry had come up with something and we wouldn't have to search half of Athens to come up with him.

When I met Larry down in the lobby I asked him, "Did you come up with anything?"

"Yeah," he said, and his whole attitude was one of disgust. "The doorman saw him leave about an hour or so ago. That was just about the time we sat down to have breakfast."

Now I knew why he felt disgusted, and I pretty much felt the same way. We hadn't been that far from Johns when he walked out of the hotel. That made us just as liable as the men upstairs on our floor.

"Now I can't rip their holes out, goddamnit," he muttered. "Shit. I'll call upstairs, Nick, and get the rest of the men down here."

"Your stringers, too, Larry," I told him, meaning the men who were not assigned to Johns personally. "We'll need all the help we can get if we're going to find him."

"Right. What about hotel security?" he asked. "You want them in on this, too?"

"No, not now," I replied. "Let's keep it in the family, Larry. Just get all of our brothers down here in a hurry, okay? We've got a hell of a lot of ground to cover."

"Does Johns know Athens at all?" he asked.

"I don't believe so, but that might make him that much harder to find." Larry frowned at me and I said, "If he doesn't know where the hell he is, how will we?"

"I gotcha."

"Was he alone when he left?" I asked.

"That's what the doorman said. You think maybe he's put himself on the block, Nick?"

"His wife says no, but I guess she could be wrong. For now, though, let's just figure that he's playing hide-and-go-seek to make a bigger pain in the ass of himself. Why don't you get those men, okay?"

"Yeah, sure," he said. As he walked to the house phone he was still muttering to himself, and I couldn't blame him. A big brain who I'm sure we all disliked had made monkeys out of all of us, and none of us were too happy about that.

Least of all me.

FIFTEEN

"Larry," I said, grabbing his arm, "did you leave a man upstairs on Mrs. Johns?"

"Oh, shit!" he snapped. "I was so pissed off about the doctor skipping out on us—"

"Okay, forget it," I told him, quickly. "Give me a man to take up there with me right now."

"Jerry," he called out, "go with Mr. Diamond. You'll stay behind to keep an eye on Mrs. Johns."

"Right," the man named Jerry said.

"Come on," I said, starting for the elevator. He had to run a few steps to catch up to me.

We didn't speak on the way up, and I felt the same kind of resentment for me radiating from him that Larry Robinson was pretending to have, only with this guy it was for real.

When we stepped out on our floor I said, "You go back to your room, I'll make sure she's still there."

"All right."

I trotted down to the door of her room and

knocked on it. It took a few moments, but she finally opened it.

"Nick," she said in surprise. She reached out to put her hand on my lapel and asked, "Did you find him, already?"

"No, not yet. We're just getting everyone together to go out and look for him. I, uh, just wanted to check and see if he had called you."

"No," she said, shaking her head, "I haven't heard a word."

"Too bad," I said. "Okay, try not to worry," I went on, touching her shoulder, "we'll find him."

"I told you before, Nick," she reminded me. "I'm not worried."

"That's right, you did tell me," I recalled. "I'll see you later."

I walked to the elevator and when she shut the door I diverted to the room used by Larry and his crew.

"She's there," I told Jerry when he answered the door.

"I know, I heard," he said.

"Don't leave this room unless she does," I instructed him.

"I'll do my job, Diamond. I don't need you to tell me how to do it. Besides, if that little doll leaves, I'll be right on her tail," he added, leering suggestively.

I poked his chest and said, "Do your job, and nothing else. Leave that girl alone, you understand?"

He looked into my eyes and saw something there that made him nod and say, "Sure, Diamond. Like I said, I'll do my job."

"Just make sure that's all you do," I advised him.

I left him standing there and took the elevator back down to the lobby. Everyone but Larry Robinson was gone.

"They're out looking," he told me when he saw the look on my face. "I sent them North, East and West. I figured we'd go down and check out Syntagma and the Plaka. It's real easy to get lost down there."

"Good choice," I said. "Let's go."

A lot of the ground we covered I had already gone over with Sherry when we'd gone sightseeing. After the morning had gone by with no luck, we all gathered back at the hotel, compared notes and then went out again to cover much the same ground.

"What if he's left Greece?" Larry asked. "What if he's on his way to China or behind the Iron Curtain?"

"I don't discount the possibility that he's here to sell himself to the highest bidder, but his wife's lived with him for three years. He's only interested in his work, Larry. The government is funding him, but there are strings. He strains against them, but he never breaks them."

"Then maybe he finally got fed up with being at the end of their string," he suggested.

"I hope not," I said, sincerely.

"Among other repercussions, our heads would definitely go rolling," he said.

He was right, but that was least on my mind at the moment. Johns taking off without warning would be like setting Sherry adrift in a rowboat with no oars.

"I hope that's not the case," I said again, "and I don't think it is."

"Why not?" he asked. We were strolling through Syntagma again with all of the tourist traffic. From there we'd go into the Plaka, which would be considerably busier in the afternoon than the morning, when we first went through it.

"He hasn't had time to set anything up, Larry. The only time he left his room was last night, and you and I both know that he didn't speak to anyone at that reception. On top of that, you've had his room bugged, so he hasn't talked to anyone on the phone, either."

"Nick, you and I both know there are ways around a bug," he pointed out.

"Yes, but Johns' specialty is weapons, not electronic bugs," I reminded him.

"He's also a genius," he argued. "How long would it take him to learn?"

"When would he have had time?"

"How long does it take to read a book?" he asked.

"Okay, okay," I surrendered. "Let's stop fencing and just hope that we're wrong."

"I'll buy that."

We entered the Plaka and it was like being on

Fifth Avenue in New York City during lunch hour.

"How the hell are we going to find him in all of this?" Larry asked.

"Where would you hide?" I asked, and he nodded and kept looking.

After an hour more of that I said, "Okay, Larry, let's check the Acropolis."

"If I have to trudge up that hill again," he threatened, "and he's not there . . ."

"Yeah, well, we'll worry about that when we get up there," I said. "Let's go."

We were halfway up the slope when we noticed somebody familiar coming down.

It was Doctor Lucas Johns.

"Shit," Larry said, staring up at the doctor. "Where the hell have you—"

He didn't finish because the sound of shots cut him off. We watched as Johns either fell or dove through the air and came tumbling down the slope toward us.

SIXTEEN

There had been two shots, and while Johns continued his downward plunge, no others followed. There were some other people coming up behind us, and a woman began to scream.

"Shit, get him!" I shouted. Larry and I both reached for him as he approached us and we each grabbed an arm successfully. Once we had him we hit the deck, waiting for further shots.

There were none.

"Doctor," Larry called out, "are you all right?"

Johns moaned and tried to move, and he had either been injured by a bullet, or the fall. Robinson and I began to examine him and we couldn't find a bullet hole, anywhere.

"Anything on your side?" I asked Larry.

"Nothing. No holes."

"Let's turn him over," I suggested. We did so, with me peering upslope and Larry looking down.

When we got him on his back we found the only damage appeared to be a cut on his head, just at his hairline.

"He must have hit his head when he hit the deck," Larry said.

"I guess so. Any ideas about where the shots came from?" I asked.

"I don't know," he said, examining Johns further. "Could have come from up top, or the bottom, I guess. Somebody with a high-powered rifle."

"With the right weapon, the shooter could have been anywhere," I said. There were any number of buildings facing the Acropolis that would have been high enough to accommodate a man with a rifle.

People around us began to move about again and I said to Larry, "We'd better get him out of here before we really draw a crowd."

"Yeah, the wrong kind."

Neither one of us wanted to have to try to explain anything to the Greek Police, so we got Johns back to his feet between us and started down the slope.

At the bottom we found a taverna and commandeered a corner table. By that time Johns had come around pretty well and we used some napkins and water to clean the blood from his face. He was still pretty filthy from his roll down the side of the hill, but we didn't really stand out all that much in a crowd, anymore.

"What the hell did you think you were doing?" Robinson demanded when Johns was lucid.

Johns looked at him with a perfectly placid expression and didn't answer.

"I'd like something to drink," he said.

Larry grabbed a full glass of water from in front of me and slapped it down in front of Johns hard enough to spill half of it.

"Drink that, Doctor," he said, "and then answer my question."

"I don't like your tone, Mr. Robinson. I will take it up with General Davies when we return home."

"You can take it up with the President for all I care, Doctor. Just what the hell were you trying to pull, skipping out like that?"

"I was suffocating, Mr. Robinson. Your security is quite tight, you know. I simply wanted to go for a walk."

"And almost get yourself killed in the process," Robinson reminded him.

"If I choose to get myself killed, Mr. Robinson, it is my choice to make."

"But it's not your choice to get us killed, too," I said.

Larry looked at me as if he were about to agree, and then remembered that we were supposed to be adversaries.

"Keep quiet, Diamond. This is between the doctor and his government, of which I happen to be the representative."

"Fine with me," I said, throwing up my hands and sitting back.

"Now, first and foremost, are you all right?" Larry asked Johns.

"I appear to be in one piece, yes. I was shot at, wasn't I?"

"You were," Robinson told him. "Now, I'd

like to know just how you got out of the hotel."

"That was simple," the doctor answered. "I walked out."

"You just . . . walked out?"

"That's correct."

"How—"

"Could I interject here for just a moment?" I asked. I tried to make Larry understand that I wanted him to let me talk. He was about to snap at me when he got the message and said, "All right, Diamond, talk."

"I think we should understand here that our whole—your whole security set-up is geared to keep people away from the doctor. In other words, you've been worried about keeping people out, and not about keeping Doctor Johns in."

"I guess that makes sense," Larry admitted, "but who the hell would have expected him to take a walk?"

"I think it's obvious now that we should have," I said.

"Yeah," Larry said. "I guess the thing to do now is make sure it doesn't happen again."

"Well, if I may say something," Johns spoke up. "I do not enjoy being shot at, and I would like to go back to the United States immediately."

"I'm afraid that's out of the question," Larry said. "We will do our best to make sure no one shoots at you again, Doctor, but you have to cooperate with us. This meeting of the minds must take place, and it starts tonight. We have to get you back to the hotel, now."

"Meeting of the minds," Johns muttered. "How is that possible when I am the only one who qualifies."

Larry and I exchanged glances and shakes of the head.

"And what about whoever shot at me?" Johns asked. "Aren't you going to find them?"

Larry looked at me and I said, "Yes, well, I'm afraid that's a whole different problem."

SEVENTEEN

"I'd like to get cleaned up, if you don't mind," Johns said to us, once we were back at his hotel room.

"And get some rest while you're at it," Larry Robinson said. "You've got a meeting to attend tonight."

"Good afternoon, dear," the doctor said to Sherry as he passed her in the doorway to the bedroom.

She stared after him, then looked back at Robinson and me and asked, "What happened?"

"He fell down," Larry said. "I'll see you later," he said to me, heading for the door.

"He fell down?" Sherry repeated.

I shrugged, "He'll tell you all about it when he comes out. I'll see you later, Sherry."

"Nick—"

"Later," I said again, and left.

EIGHTEEN

I went back to my room and used some special equipment from the false bottom in my suitcase to modify my TV set into a communications device. Once that was done, I got David Hawk on the line and filled him in on what had been going on since my arrival in Athens.

"Are you working well with Larry Robinson?" he asked.

"Very well, sir. We've worked together before."

"Good. Just make sure he doesn't slip and give your identity away to the Johns."

"He won't. Larry's a good man."

"I'll take your word for that, N3. What about these attempts on Doctor and Mrs. Johns. Any theories?"

"Might be the same people involved, sir. A couple of pros might have been able to get Mrs. Johns away from me, and a pro would have nailed the doctor on that slope."

"Then you feel you are dealing with amateurs."

"At the operational level, anyway. Whoever is doing the planning might be trying to make do with what he can get."

"And who do you think that might be?"

I hesitated a moment, then said, "I'm not sure yet, sir. Robinson feels that the doctor's disappearing act might have something to do with trying to sell his services to another government."

"And how do you feel about that?"

"I don't think that's the case, sir, but don't ask me why. It's just a feeling I have."

He hesitated a moment, and then said, "I won't push you, N3. Your instincts have always seemed to serve you quite well in the past."

"Thank you, sir."

"Is there anything I can do to help?"

"As a matter of fact, there is," I said, and then went on to tell him just what I wanted done back in Washington.

"What are we trying to find?" he asked, after my explanation.

"Uh, I think you'll know when you find it, sir."

"Very well, N3," he sighed. "You will keep in touch so I can give you the results of the search?"

"I'll be in touch, sir."

"Good luck, N3."

"Thank you, sir."

I dismantled my communications device, then retrieved the half-full bottle of bourbon I'd ordered the night before.

First an attempt to snatch Sherry, and now an apparent attempt to blow the doctor away. What I had told Hawk was very true, though. Had these attempts been made by pros, either one could have been brought off successfully.

The only problem now was that whoever was doing the planning might realize that and bring in some pros to work with. We were going to have to keep the doctor and his wife very close to the hotel from now on while we tried to figure out who was behind the two attempts that had been made—so far!

It had to be one of the countries who was attending the meeting. They must have felt that it would serve their country greatly if Doctor Lucas Johns were to die. The attempt to snatch Sherry might have been a ruse to draw the doctor out of the hotel.

But who was behind it, that was the question.

And what could we do to find out?

NINETEEN

On second thought, I took the bourbon bottle with me and went down the hall to Robinson's room. When I knocked he answered himself and I extended the bottle to him.

"What's this?" he asked.

"A peace offering," I said in an unnaturally loud voice.

He laughed and said, "Come on in, Nick. There's no one else here."

"Oh," I said, grateful that we'd be able to speak freely. I went in and shut the door behind me.

"I'll get a couple of glasses," he said. "Would you like me to call room service for some ice?"

"Not on my account," I answered.

He came back with the glasses and I poured us three fingers each.

"What's on your mind?"

"Same thing that's on yours," I said.

"Yeah," he drawled, "keeping that pain in the

ass alive so he can go into that meeting tonight and snub and insult the representatives of four other countries."

"Very well put."

"Thank you."

I passed him the bottle and he freshened his drink.

"I think we've got to think offensively about this, Larry," I offered.

"I think the doctor is offensive enough for all of us," Larry replied.

"No, I'm serious about this, Larry."

He put down his glass and said, "Okay, then, let's talk about it seriously."

"We can't just sit back and wait for whoever's out there to take another shot at Doctor Johns and his wife. We've got to make an attempt to figure out who it is that's behind it."

"How do we do that?"

"I don't know. Let's keep an eye on the people at the meeting, tonight. Maybe somebody will be surprised to see Johns alive and in attendance."

"Okay," he agreed. "You think it's one of them?"

"Maybe not one of the esteemed doctors," I said. "Maybe it's their security people. The Russians or the Germans."

"Top of the list, huh?"

"Well, we can concentrate on them while not ruling out the French and British altogether. Tell you what, I'll watch the Russians and the British, you take the others."

I poured myself another drink and looked around the room. I spotted the electronic equipment just a couple of feet away from me, and the needle was jumping, indicating that there was a conversation, or at least some noise, going on in the Johns' room.

"Larry," I called out.

"Yeah?"

I indicated the jumping needle and said, "Let's give a listen, huh?"

"Sure," he said. He reached over and flicked a switch.

". . . can't do something like this again, Lucas," Sherry was saying.

"I can do whatever I like, my dear," her husband countered.

"You owe something to the government, Lucas, whether you want to admit it or not," she argued.

"No, you're wrong!" he said loudly. "I owe them nothing, and I don't need you to try and tell me that I'm wrong. You haven't the capabilities to even try to correct me, Sherry, dear. Remember that you are an ornament, nothing more."

I winced when I heard him say that, so I could imagine how she must have felt.

"Oh, Lucas . . ."

"Don't give me any tears, darling. They have no effect on me, you know."

"Lucas, when did you get so cruel?"

"When I found out what a slut you are," he answered.

"You call me a slut because I asked you for a little love when we were first married?"

"I thought you were different," he said. "I saw the way you cringed when those men touched you, and I thought you were different from the others."

"What others?"

"The ones who want only sex," he explained, "the sluts in this world."

"Lucas, if I cringed when men touched me three years ago, it wasn't because they were men, it was because they weren't the right . . . man."

"And you thought I was the right man? You thought I would touch you?"

"Lucas, why did you marry me?" she cried out.

"I married you because I thought you understood, I thought you would never ask anything else from me. I thought you knew that my work was everything, and that I had no time for anything else."

"Lucas . . ." she said, looking for words, "I'm . . . sorry . . ."

"Don't apologize," he told her. "I'm going to soak in a hot tub. I'm a bit sore from my fall."

"Lucas, you didn't tell me about the fall. How did it happen?" she asked.

"You really care, don't you?" he asked.

"Of course I care. You don't live with someone for three years and not care," she said. When there was no answer she said, "Do you, Lucas?"

After a long silence, Johns' voice said, "I'm going to bathe. Why don't you rest before we have to go."

There were some other sounds that were not readily identifiable, and then Larry leaned over and shut the machine off.

"Wow," he said.

"That explains a few things," I said, only half aloud.

"There's something wrong with that man," Larry observed, "that much is obvious."

"Yes, I guess it is," I said, wondering how Sherry must have felt at that moment.

"Well, I guess we've come up with the only plan possible," Larry said. "We watch."

"That'll have to do for now," I agreed. I stood up to leave and Larry said, "Uh, are you going to take that bottle with you?"

There wasn't that much left, so I handed it to him.

"What are you going to do now?" he asked.

"We covered a lot of ground today," I said. "I'm going to clean up and get some rest. I want to be alert this evening."

"Good idea. I'll see you later."

"Let me know when you're going to go for the doctor," I said.

"Will do, Nick."

I left his room and stood out in the hall, toying with the idea of knocking on Sherry's door while her husband was in the bath, but I decided against it. I went back to my own room, took a shower and then a nap.

I wanted to be especially alert that evening.

TWENTY

We entered the main lounge with Lucas and Sherry Johns in the center, Larry Robinson on their right and me on their left. I was standing next to Sherry and every so often she would brush against me, as if seeking some kind of solace, or strength, from the contact.

Once the five principals went into the convention meeting room, I'd have a chance to take her somewhere and talk, alone, and at the same time make sure nothing happened to her.

"I have to go and confer with the other heads of security," Larry told us. "Stay here." He turned to two of his men and told them not to leave the Johns for any reason.

"This is ridiculous," Johns said while we waited.

"Be tolerant, Doctor," I said.

He stared at me and said, "I don't need advice in tolerance from a bodyguard, Diamond."

I stared back at him and was about to make a sharp retort when Larry Robinson came back.

"Okay, here's how it goes down," he told us.

"I go in with the other four heads of security to check out the room, and then the five of you go in, Doctor."

"I go in with you," I told Larry. He looked at me, frowned, and before he could reply I added, "It's my job, Mr. Robinson."

"I don't know if they'll go along with it," he said, doubtfully.

"They will either go along with it," Doctor Johns said in a low, even voice, "or they will hold their little tête-à-tête without me."

Robinson and Johns exchanged glances this time, and then Larry said, "Wait here."

He went over and talked to his four counterparts, who looked over at me as he spoke. Diana Ridgeway, who looked especially fetching that night, also glanced my way. She had traded in her hard-lined suit for something softer, and all her curves—as well as her knees—showed.

Robinson came back with a grim look on his face. "Do you know your job?" he asked me, obviously for the doctor's benefit.

"I know it."

"Doctor, they won't go for it," he said to Johns. "Not both of us. One or the other. The choice would appear to be yours."

"In that case," Johns said, and then turned to me, "in you go, Diamond."

Robinson made the appropriate noises, but in the end he brought me over and introduced me to the others.

"This is Mr. Diamond. He is Doctor Johns' personal security man. He will check the room out with you."

The others nodded, and the Russian said, "We are ready."

"Let's go," I said.

The five of us went into the room and instead of checking it together, we all wandered around, checking for bombs and bugs and anything else that shouldn't be there. Eventually, we all covered the same ground and met back at the door.

"Looks clean to me," I told them.

"Is clean," the Russian, Mikel Destrovitch, agreed.

"Ja," the German, von Klemperer chimed in.

"Oui," little Georges Duprée added.

Mount, the Englishman, was the last to join us, and he stuck his chin up and said, "Everything seems tiptop."

"Super," I said, and he frowned at me.

We went back out and gave our people the all clear sign.

"You can go in, Doctor," Robinson told Johns.

"Can I really?" Johns asked, grimacing. "Shit! Diamond, you'll see to Mrs. Johns, won't you?"

"Yes, sir, I will."

"Yes, I thought you would," he said. He gave Sherry and myself prolonged looks, and then walked into the meeting room. Diana Ridgeway was the last to enter, not one to stand on formality, and she turned and gave me a look, as well, although hers was quite different.

"Now what?" I asked Larry.

"Now the rest of us will simply wait out here," he said.

"Well, not me," I said. "I'll leave him in your very capable hands. All you spy types should be able to keep the riff-raff out," I said, adding, "if you don't shoot each other, that is."

I took Sherry's arm and said, "Come on, let's get some dinner."

"All right," she agreed.

Larry nodded at me behind her back and I threw him a wink.

"Where would you like to eat?" I asked her.

"I don't care," she said, dully.

"Then we'll try the roof again. Okay?"

"I don't care," she said again.

I steered her to the elevator and we went to the roof. When we were settled in at a table I ordered for the both of us, and told the waiter to bring drinks right away.

"You want to talk about it?" I asked her.

"About what?" she asked.

I hesitated while the waiter put down our drinks and a plate of *tomates yemistes me risi*—an hors d'oeuvres of tomatoes stuffed with rice.

"About whatever happened this afternoon," I said after the waiter had gone.

She stared down at the table for a few moments and then out at the Tomb of the Unknown Soldier.

"We had a fight," she said, "or a discussion, I should say. Lucas never fights, he discusses."

"What did you discuss?"

"Why he married me; what I was. He told me I was a slut."

"Did you tell him about—"

"No, of course I didn't tell him. He just said I was a slut, like the rest of them."

"The rest of who?" I asked, although I knew.

"Women," she said. "He's the opposite of you, Nick. You think so much of women, and Lucas thinks so little."

I took her hand and said, "Then there's something wrong with him, Sherry. Feel sorry for him, yes, but don't let it make you so miserable."

Her eyes filled with tears, but she didn't let them fall. "You're right, Nick," she said, holding hands with me tightly. She looked down at her appetizer with an expression that was considerably more cheerful than the one she had been wearing when we got there. "This does look delicious."

"Well, go ahead and dig in, then. Dinner will be here soon enough."

She attacked the tomato with gusto, and then paused as if a thought had struck her. "Nick?"

"Yes?"

"Do you think they'll be in that meeting long?"

"They should be, Sherry."

"Long enough for us to go back to your room after dinner?" she asked, hopefully.

I smiled and said, "Yeah, at least that long."

TWENTY-ONE

I hugged her tightly and took advantage of the position it put us in to look at my watch. We had skipped dessert and went right to my room after dinner. I understood the hurt and emptiness Sherry was feeling and made love to her tenderly, but now I was acutely aware of the time.

"Getting late," I said. "Do you want to wait in your room or go down and meet him?"

"I'll wait in the room," she said.

"Okay, then you better get dressed and get over there now. They've been down there a few hours, and I don't think anybody can take more than that of Doctor Lucas Johns the first time out."

She made a face, but obediently got to her feet and began to get dressed. When she was ready to leave, she walked over to the bed and said, "Don't get up, Nick." She kissed me shortly and headed for the door.

"If you need anything," I called after her, "just knock on the wall."

"I will," she said. "I'll see you tomorrow, Nick."

After she left I thought about calling downstairs

for one of Larry's men to come up and watch Sherry so I could go down and spend some time in the lounge with the other security people, but then I decided against it. Robinson was the American security chief and the others might not feel free to talk around me.

Earlier, in the lounge, I had watched the faces of the English and Russian security people, as well as the faces of the very people they were there to protect, and I had seen no sign of surprise or shock. I'd have to wait for Larry to come back up before I could find out what he had seen in the faces of the Frenchman DuPrée, or the German von Klemperer. Hopefully, he would have been able to spot something, otherwise we were going to be right back at square one. I would hate to have been forced into waiting for whoever it was to make another try. Waiting for something to happen always makes me nervous.

So now I had something else to think about. How could I go about making something happen here in Athens? There were only two choices, and one appealed to me even less than the other.

The first was to use Doctor Johns as bait, but if he got killed, the United States government wouldn't be very happy with me.

The second was to use Sherry. The government wouldn't get very upset if Sherry were killed . . . but I sure as hell would.

What bothered me was that I'd probably use Sherry because that's what I'd have to do to get the job done.

I got up and got dressed because I wanted to talk to Robinson as soon as I heard them all come back up. I also called room service for another bottle of bourbon.

The level in the Early Times bottle was down a third by the time I heard the elevator stop at the eighth floor. I waited until I heard Johns walk by and open his door before picking up the phone and dialing Robinson's room.

"Larry, Nick," I said. "How did it go?"

"They wanted to tear him apart," he said, sounding out of breath, as if he'd had to physically restrain them from doing just that. "He's got them all against him, Nick."

"Against him?" I asked. "How bad, Larry?"

"I don't mean that, Nick. It's just that he opposed every proposal the others made. He already has the meeting stymied."

"Okay, I guess that's something they're going to have to work out among themselves," I said. "What about the security people. Did you notice anything when we walked in? Did they say anything while you were all waiting for tonight's meeting to break up?"

"I didn't see much when we walked in, Nick," he said, sounding tired, "and they didn't say a hell of a lot afterward."

"Yeah, I didn't pick anything up," I said. "As a matter of fact, they're a pretty goddamned stone-faced bunch."

"Yep, and they talk just about as much," he agreed. "Listen, Nick, I'm really bushed. Can we huddle on this in the morning, maybe over breakfast?"

"In the morning, yeah," I agreed, "but maybe not over breakfast. I'll let you know, okay?"

"Sure."

We hung up and I wondered what the hell I'd gotten dressed for. I took off my jacket and threw it down on a chair, then poured some more bourbon into a glass. In spite of myself, I started straining to hear if there was some kind of conversation going on in the next room. Sherry certainly had time to shower and fall asleep before Johns showed up.

I finished the bourbon and started to think about getting some sleep for myself when somebody started pounding on my door.

"Who is it?" I asked. I walked to the door and stood off to one side.

"It's Doctor Johns, Diamond. Open up!" he shouted, sounding more upset than I'd ever heard him.

"Sure, Doctor," I called out. I kept my hand on Wilhelmina as I opened the door, and relaxed when I saw that he was alone.

"What's the problem?" I asked.

"Where is she?" he demanded, walking past me. When he brushed by me, I gave way on purpose, or he wouldn't have been able to do so.

"Where's who?" I asked.

"Sherry. Don't think I don't know what's been going on, Diamond," he said, turning on me.

"And don't think you're the first. That little slut—"

"Hold it, Johns," I snapped back. "Sherry's not a slut and she's not here. Are you telling me that she's not in your room?"

"That's what I'm telling you," he said. "Sherry's gone!"

TWENTY-TWO

I left him standing there staring accusingly and ran over to his room, the door to which he had left open. I went through the apartment quickly. I didn't find Sherry, and I didn't find any signs that she might have been taken by force.

Johns came in behind me, muttering about how we thought he was a fool. "Stay here," I told him, and ran down the hall to start pounding on Robinson's door. One of his men answered and I said, "Get Robinson and bring him down the hall to Johns' room."

"Hey, pal—"

I poked him in the chest and I said, "Do it now! Mrs. Johns is missing."

"Jesus—" he began, but I didn't wait for the rest. I went back down the hall and found Johns standing exactly as I'd left him.

Robinson was the first man through the door behind me, wearing pants and a tee shirt. "Did I hear right?" he asked.

"Yeah," I said, "she's gone."

He stuck his head out the door and told two of

his men to get right down to the lobby and see if they could find her.

"She didn't walk out alone, Larry," I told him.

"Just covering all bases, Nick. Any sign of a struggle?"

"None, but I'm certain—fairly certain—that she wouldn't have left her room to go for a walk. Not without telling me."

Both Johns and Robinson gave me curious looks, but I ignored them.

Robinson instructed two of his other men to look through the apartment again. He grabbed the phone and said, "I'll call my stringers and get them out looking, too."

I stood there, shaking my head. "I don't think she's going to walk into our arms like her husband did, Larry."

At the mention of her husband Robinson gave me a warning look, but I was beyond worrying about keeping our acquaintance a secret from the doctor. In fact, I wasn't even worried about the doctor anymore at that moment.

"Forget it," I said to Larry.

He shrugged his shoulders and continued dialing.

"Hank, it's Robinson. Get the boys on the street, we're looking for Mrs. Johns," he said into the phone. "We don't know, but chances are she didn't just take a walk. Meet me downstairs in a half an hour."

He hung up and looked at me with his hands on his hips. His two men came back to the front door and one of them said, "Nothing, Robby."

"Okay. Get downstairs, I'll meet you there. Dave, you stay in the room."

Both men nodded and left.

Robinson was studying me, and I knew he had a question he wanted to ask.

"Sit down, Doctor," I said to Johns, who hadn't yet spoken a word. "Over there," I added, pointing to an armchair across the room. He stood there for a few seconds, and then turned, walked to the chair and sat.

"What?" I said to Robinson.

"What do you mean?"

"Come on, Larry, you've got a question burning to come out. Give it to me."

He rubbed his jaw and studied my face a little longer, then threw up his hands. "All right, Nick," he said, too low for Johns to hear from where he was. "How? How did they get into her room and get her out with you right next door?"

I knew that was what he wanted to ask, because I had been asking myself the same question for the last few minutes.

How the hell could someone have come up on the elevator, gotten into her room, grabbed her and taken her back down the elevator without my having heard a blessed thing?

I knew I hadn't fallen asleep since she'd left my room, so there was only one answer.

"They didn't," I replied.

"What?"

"They didn't get in while I was next door," I

said. "That's the only answer, Larry."

"What's the only answer, Nick?" he asked, still puzzled.

"Larry, while we were all downstairs in the lounge, there was nobody up here, was there?"

"Ah, no, I don't think so."

"So when I brought her back up here and she went into her room, somebody was already in there waiting for her. Nobody got into this room while I was next door."

He thought it over a moment, then came up with a blockbuster of an answer.

"Okay, Nick, that answers half of the question. The fact remains, they still got her out without you hearing them. Explain that."

I was afraid I didn't have an answer—yet.

TWENTY-THREE

"The tape!" I said, suddenly.

"What?"

"The bug. It must have picked something up. Let's get back to your room and listen."

We left Johns' room and walked down the hall to Robinson's. Johns continued to keep his mouth shut, but he trailed along with us.

When he realized what we were doing, however, he started to get huffy, again.

"My God," he declared, "you've bugged my room! How dare you. Of all the—" he was going on, but when I turned and looked at him he stopped and leaned against the wall, watching us.

"Play it," I told Robinson. "Go back about half an hour."

"Half an hour?" he asked, looking surprised. "Is that all? You left the lounge at . . ." his voice trailed off as he put a few things together and got the picture.

He rewound the tape and started to play it.

There was nothing but silence for a few minutes, then the sound of a door opening and . . . static!

"Shit," he said. We let it run a little further, but it was useless.

"Okay, shut it," I said.

Robinson let some air out through his mouth and said, "Whoever it was had a jammer on him. He either knew or assumed that we'd have the room wired."

"Yeah," I said, running my thumbnail along my bottom lip. "All right, here's how it plays so far for me. See if you agree. The guy waits for all of us to leave the floor. He comes up, gets in with a key or a lockpick, then activates the jammer in his pocket. He sits and waits . . . for what?"

"For the doctor and/or his wife to come back," Larry answered.

"But how can he be sure that one or the other will come back alone?" I asked. "How does he know that both won't show up with four security men?"

Larry shrugged and said, "Maybe he just figured to get lucky."

"I don't think so," I said, but I didn't elaborate.

"Do you think this is connected with the other two attempts?"

"What other two attempts?" Johns asked, getting brave again. "I thought you said that you and Sherry were mugged?"

"Shut up, Doctor," I said.

"Look, Diamond, you work for me," the doctor

said, walking over to us. "That is, you did. You're fired." Johns turned to Robinson and said, "Mr. Robinson, I now place myself solely in your hands."

"Shut up, Johns," Larry told him, and Johns shut up. He didn't know what else to do.

"Go back to your room, Doctor," I instructed him.

"But—but if Sherry is really missing, if someone has really taken her, I will be protected, won't I?"

I stared at him and thought back. He hadn't been that upset when he got shot at by the Acropolis. Why was he so shook up now?

"Go back to your room, Doctor," Larry repeated for me. "You'll be amply protected, I assure you."

Johns looked doubtful, but he turned and walked down the hall to his own room. I walked to the door and when I heard his door close and the lock click, I shut Robinson's.

"When he gets his nerve back, he's going to scream," Robinson said. "Davies is going to chew my ass."

"I'll have my boss talk to him," I said. "Don't worry about it. Let's worry about this girl, okay?"

Larry frowned and asked, "Have you got something going with her, Nick?"

"I like her, Larry, that's all. She deserves to be somewhere else, with someone else."

"I can't argue with that."

"You're supposed to meet your men downstairs," I reminded him.

"Oh, yeah," he said. He reset the listening device and then stood up. "For her sake, Nick, I hope she just went for a walk."

"I wish that was it, Larry. I wish that was the case, but I've had a bad feeling and that business with the jammer locks it up."

He shrugged his shoulders and said, "Maybe there was a short in the wiring, who knows?"

"Who knows," I repeated. I walked over to the box and hit a toggle switch. Johns' voice came over loud and clear as he cursed me, Robinson and the entire U.S. government for trying to make a fool out of him. He was really worried about his wife.

I shut the switch, turned to Robinson and said, "We know."

He nodded shortly and put his hand on the doorknob. "I've got to meet my men."

"Hey, Larry."

"What?" he asked.

"You better put your shirt on."

TWENTY-FOUR

I remained in Robinson's room for a while after he left, trying to fit some pieces together in my mind. At one point I decided to go back to my room just long enough to get the new bottle of bourbon.

I was about to enter my room when a thought struck me, and I removed Wilhelmina from my holster.

What if Sherry and whoever snatched her had not left this floor yet? I hadn't heard the elevator at all, that had to be it.

We had the whole floor for our "convention," but we didn't have enough people to fill all of the rooms. Consequently, there were a few empty rooms between each of the rooms occupied by the other representatives. We seemed to be further away from the others than they were from each other. Doctor Johns' doing, no doubt.

I retraced my steps back to Robinson's room. Once inside I started looking for a floor plan of the floor we were on. There had to be a master, to show where each representative and his security crew were placed.

I finally found it, tacked to a large board and propped facing a wall. I turned it around and studied it.

Now I knew why I had heard very little elevator activity the entire time we'd been here. The other reps had been placed so that it made more sense for them to use another elevator bank.

I should have realized there'd be more than one elevator on the floor.

Whoever had taken Sherry could just as well have come up on the other elevator, thereby avoiding being heard by me.

But not by others.

And what if Sherry were being held in one of the other security apartments?

Her disappearance was shaping up to be more than just puzzling. There was a possible international incident in the works. When Larry Robinson came back, as head of American security, he was going to have to speak to the other security personnel about looking through their quarters. I couldn't approach their security force, because to them I was simply Doctor Johns' personal bodyguard, with no authority to act for my government.

I propped the layout back against the wall, and began searching the empty rooms.

TWENTY-FIVE

With Wilhelmina in hand, I started picking the locks on the empty rooms and checking them, one by one. There were forty-six rooms on our floor, and thirty-six of them were unoccupied. There were five rooms for the five delegates and five rooms for each of their security heads and their immediate bodyguards. The stringers were in rooms on other floors, above and below us.

Most of those rooms were just that, rooms and not suites. It was necessary only to open the door and flick the light switch to ascertain whether or not they were empty. I did, however, take the time to check closets and bathrooms, on the off chance that Sherry might have been tied up and left in one.

I had checked the rooms on our side of the floor and was about to start working my way down another hall when the elevator doors opened and Larry Robinson and three of his men exited.

"Larry," I called, moving down the hall toward them.

When he saw me he held his hand out and said, "Nothing, Nick."

"I came up with an idea," I said, explaining my thoughts.

"You want me to ask the other security heads if we can search their rooms, and the rooms of their people?"

"Yes."

He gave me an odd look and said, "That's a longshot, Nick."

"Let's give it a try, Larry. Also, the British security people have the room closest to the other elevator bank. Ask them if there was anyone in their room while we were downstairs. If there was, maybe they heard something."

"I think we were all downstairs, Nick," he said.

"Come on, Larry, ask, for crying out loud. We've got to do what we can."

"All right, Nick, all right. Take it easy." He turned and gave his men instructions. One he told to stay in the room, another to go back downstairs and wait for the others to come back. The third man was given one of the hallways and the numbers of the empty rooms.

"I'll check with the British security people, and then check the empty rooms along their hallway. After that I'll talk to the Russian, German and French security."

"All right," I said. "I'll check that far hall, and then I'm going to talk to Diana Ridgeway."

"What for?"

"She likes me, I think she'll talk to me. Maybe

I can get her to exert some pressure on her security people, and maybe even the other delegates. God knows, they wouldn't lift a finger if Johns asked them."

"And I don't think he'd ask them, anyway."

I nodded and said, "Okay, let's get started."

We each went off on our appointed rounds and I reminded them to be careful. If we found Sherry Johns, we might also find whoever had taken her.

I was pretty damned sure that whoever that turned out to be would not like being found.

TWENTY-SIX

I didn't find a thing until I picked the lock on the last of my empty rooms.

The last one wasn't empty.

"I beg your pardon?" the woman said in a slight Russian accent.

When I got over my surprise at finding someone in the room, I recognized who she was. She was the handsome woman who had been in the lounge with Doctor Boris Ravinsky, the Russian who thought he was a ladies man.

"I'm sorry," I said. I was prepared to allay any fears she might have had from finding a strange man in her room, but she seemed to be taking it quite well.

Even though she was totally naked.

She had a handsome body to go with the face. Proud breasts that were not as firm as they used to be, but still quite nice, topped by cherry nipples. There was a slight roll of extra flesh around her once trim waist, but not enough to ruin the view. She was well put together for a woman who must have been in her early to middle forties.

"I know you," she said, pointing a finger at me. In her other hand she held a small towel, but made no effort to try and hide her nudity behind it. "You were at the reception last night with the American doctor."

"Please, don't be frightened," I said. I had assumed that since she was with Ravinsky, they would be sharing a room. Obviously, Robinson had thought so, also, because his chart showed this room as being empty.

"Oh, I am not frightened, comrade," she said. "In fact, I am pleasantly surprised."

"You are?"

She nodded and said, "Yes, indeed. I thought that all of your attention had been taken up by that English lady, the one who looks like ice."

"Diana Ridgeway."

"Yes. Apparently, you noticed me after all, eh? My name is Natasha," she supplied, removing a damp ringlet of hair from her forehead. The movement raised her breasts and her nipples looked as if they were hardening. I wondered if that wasn't a reaction to the cool air on her damp body.

"Uh, Natasha, yes, I did notice you."

"Relax, handsome man," she said. "I will put on my robe, yes? And then you can tell me what you are here for."

When she came back she was belting a silk robe and her nipples were very apparent beneath the silk. "Is this better?" she asked, laughing.

"Only just."

"Please, sit down and tell me your name."

"Diamond, Nick Diamond, Miss—"

"Just Natasha," she said. "So, what are you doing in my room?"

I looked into her eyes and I liked her, so I decided to play it straight with her. I told her about the disappearance of Doctor Johns' wife and that I was checking unassigned rooms.

"I thought this was an empty room," I ended.

"We decided on separate rooms at the last moment," she explained. "I am sorry about the doctor's wife. He must be very worried for her."

"Yes," I lied, "he is."

"Why would you think that she was in an empty room?" she asked.

"Natasha, there's a possibility that she didn't leave her room of her own free will."

"Ah, and you thought that perhaps you would find her in an empty room, tied up somehow?"

"That's right."

"I understand," she said. "All this security. My country is also very worried about Boris. He would not come unless they allowed me to come, also, but they would not take responsibility for my safety. But, I am not married to him."

"I see."

"I would not *be* married to him," she said. "He would drive me crazy with his countless women. Ah!" She waved her hands, as if shooing away the very idea of being married to Boris Ravinsky. "Do not worry," she told me suddenly. "I will not complain about you breaking into my room."

"That's very kind of you," I answered.

"You may look around if you like," she said.

"You wouldn't be insulted?"

"Look around, Nick, and then I will tell you what *would* offend me," she said.

I made a quick check of the suite, including the bathroom and the closets, and found nothing.

"Satisfied?"

"Yes, Natasha," I replied. "You've been very kind about this."

"Kind," she said, waving the word away. "I am a selfish and spoiled woman."

"What is it that would offend you?" I asked, curiously.

"Ah," she said, standing up and taking my arm. Walking me to the door she said, "I would be very insulted if you broke into my room and did not even attempt to steal a kiss."

I smiled and looked at her mouth. She had very inviting lips, and I leaned down to taste them. She locked her hands around my neck and gave me much more than a little taste.

"I will not complain," she said again, "on one condition."

"Condition?" I asked. "What is it?"

"You must promise to come back when you have found the missing woman."

I looked at her and said, "I'll try."

She smiled and said, "I will take that as a promise, Nicholas. Good luck."

"Thank you, Natasha."

"You are very welcome, my handsome American," she said, letting her hands slide down my chest. "You are very, very welcome."

Any other time, I told myself, leaving her room.

As I turned to go down the hall I saw Diana Ridgeway standing in front of her door, fitting the key into the lock. She was about four rooms away, and the rooms between hers and the one I'd just left were empty.

"Well," she said. We were alone in the hallway and her voice carried very well.

"Well, what?" I asked.

She gave me a crooked smile and said, "Well, if you're looking for my room, it's this one."

She opened her door and stepped in, but I could tell from the light in the hall that she'd left the door open behind her. As I walked down the hall toward her room, I couldn't shake the feeling that I was going from the frying pan to the fire.

TWENTY-SEVEN

When I walked into Diana Ridgeway's room and closed the door behind me she was pouring brandy into two glasses.

"I thought your drink was scotch?" I asked.

"This is just to help me . . . relax," she said. She walked across the room and handed me one of the glasses.

"What were you doing out of your room this late at night?" I asked her.

"*Mmm*," she said, into her glass. "Now you sound just like my security people. Why don't you drink your brandy and relax, too?" she asked.

"I wish I could relax, Doctor Ridgeway, but I can't. Not now."

"Do I at least have time to get more comfortable?" she asked. She was wearing the same dress she had worn when I first saw her earlier that evening.

"Sure," I said.

"Sit down and wait," she said, putting her glass down on an end table. "I won't be long."

When she returned from her bedroom, she was wearing nothing more than an expectant look. Her breasts were incredibly full and firm; the nipples, large and pale brown, were already distended with anticipation.

"Tell me I was wrong in thinking we were . . . alike, somehow," she said, sounding like she was daring me.

I wanted her cooperation, and I didn't think she would take my refusal of her physical charms as well as Natasha had. A woman like Diana Ridgeway would see that as simple rejection and would not take kindly to it.

I approached her, took her in my arms and kissed her. The kiss lasted a very long time and when we broke she was breathless.

"I guess I wasn't wrong, was I?" she asked.

"I guess not."

TWENTY-EIGHT

"A little rushed," she said, "but very nice, Nick. You've got something on your mind, though, don't you."

"You're a sharp lady, Diana," I said. I propped myself up on one elbow and said, "Yes, as a matter of fact, there is something on my mind, and maybe you can help me."

"I will if I can, luv," she said.

I gave it to her straight, and while she listened I watched her face and knew I'd played it right. If I had turned her down she wouldn't have listened, but now she was all ears and very eager to be of some help.

"I'll talk to my people," she said, "but we'd have no reason to kidnap Johns' wife, Nick. I'd put a few bob on the Russians or the Germans."

"I'd tend to agree, Diana, but we've got to cover all bets," I explained.

"I understand, dear," she said, tracing circles over my abdomen with her nails.

I checked my watch and said, "I've got to

touch base with Robinson."

"The American security chief?" she asked. "A rather sour-looking young man, isn't he?"

"Oh, I don't know," I said, sitting up.

"Must you go?" she asked, wrapping her fingers around my forearm.

"I'm afraid so, Diana. Once this is all cleared up, I'm sure we'll have more time to . . . try and get it right."

"Oh, I didn't say it wasn't right," she corrected me, lying back down in bed, "I just said it was too fast. Then again, luv, the orgasm hasn't been invented yet that is long enough for me."

Pulling on my pants and surreptitiously securing Pierre to my right thigh once again, I said, "I get the feeling you could be hazardous to a man's health."

"You're sweet to say so," she said, laughing.

When I was fully dressed I said, "I appreciate your help on this, Diana."

"Why don't I call the dour Mr. Mount before you leave," she said suddenly, sitting up and reaching for the phone.

"All right," I said.

She dialed his room and said, "John, this is Diana. Yes, I'm quite fine, thank you. John, has the American security man, Mr. Robinson been to see you yet? He's there now? Yes, I know why he's there, John. I would like you to cooperate with him, please. Let him look around your room." She smiled at me and nodded.

"Ask him about the elevator," I said.

When she hung up she told me, "John said he didn't leave anyone in the room."

"Neither did we. It looks like a lot of negligence has contributed to this problem. I've got to go, Diana. I'm very grateful—"

"Save it for when you're finished with your work," she told me. "Then come back and show me how slowly you can be grateful."

"You've got a date."

I kissed her and left to find Larry Robinson.

TWENTY-NINE

I met Larry Robinson in the hall.

"Nothing in any of the empties," he said.

"None here, either," I said, not bothering to mention anything about the Russian woman, Natasha. "Any luck with the other security people?"

"Let's go back to my room," he suggested. "We'll talk about it there."

I nodded and started for his room. Along the way we ran into the man who had been checking the other empty rooms, and he reported the same results.

"Go downstairs, then, and see what they've come up with," Robinson instructed him.

"Yes, sir," the man said, and took the elevator down.

When we entered his room I checked the needle on the listening device and it was moving very little. It wouldn't have surprised me to turn up the sound and find Johns still muttering to himself.

I sat on the couch and asked Robinson, "What did the others say?"

He made a face and shook his head.

"Whatever you said—or did—to the English lady did the trick. I got a look at their room, and the French also let me look in theirs. I got a lot of dirty looks, but didn't find a thing."

I waited for him to continue, and when he didn't I said, "And?"

"And . . . the Russians and the Germans wouldn't go for it. They threatened all kinds of reprisals, not the least of which was withdrawing from this meeting."

"That much we figured," I commented.

"Yeah. Look, Nick, I'm going to have to call home on this. I've got to find out how hard they want us to push."

"I can tell you that," I said. He looked at me and I continued. "We push as hard as we have to to find Sherry Johns."

"Nick, I can't push us right into an international incident," he argued.

"Larry, we *have* an international incident. The wife of a prominent American scientist has disappeared at an international summit meeting in Athens, Greece. You can't get any more international than that."

"Still, I'd better make the call."

"I think maybe we should look at the reasons why Mrs. Johns might have been taken."

"All right," he agreed. "Make some suggestions."

"Well, the obvious one is ransom."

"You mean, you think the Russians or the Germans have taken her with intentions of collecting a ransom? It doesn't make sense."

"Just bear with me a few moments."

"Okay, okay, go ahead," he said, seating himself in a chair.

"Whoever has her is going to try and lure Doctor Johns out of the hotel and away from our protection so they can either snatch him or kill him, or they are actually going to demand a ransom."

"If it's the first," Larry contributed, "we'd have to vote for the Russians and Germans, but if it's the second, it could be anybody."

"That's right."

Shaking his head he said, "Nick, I've got to make the call."

"All right," I said, surrendering, "make your call, Larry. I'll be in my room. Let me know how it turns out."

"I will."

When I left him he was picking up the phone to call home, I assumed to speak to General Davies.

I went back to my room to make a call of my own—to David Hawk!

THIRTY

"It sounds like things have pretty much gotten out of control," Hawk said when I explained the situation to him.

"I wouldn't exactly put it that way, sir," I said.

"No," he replied "*you* wouldn't. Doctor Johns is bound to be wondering right now if you aren't a little more than what you appear to be."

"I'd have to agree with that, sir," I answered, "but let him wonder."

"That's up to you, N3. You tell him as much as you feel is necessary. I'll talk to General Davies and find out how he intends to tell his man to handle it. I know I don't need to tell you that great care is needed when dealing with the Russians and the Germans."

"I know that, sir. Uh, did you get a chance to do what I asked you to do?"

"Yes, we did," he replied. "It was necessary to dig up Doctor Johns' garden, but we did manage to find a twin barrel, sawed-off shotgun buried there. Do you want particulars?"

"That's not necessary, sir," I said. As long as it was there, I wasn't concerned with make or model. "And whose fingerprints were found on the weapon?" I asked.

"There was only one set of prints on the shotgun, N3. As you expected, they belong to Doctor Johns."

"Yes, sir, I did expect that. Thank you."

"Keep in touch, N3 . . . and tread carefully when dealing with our foreign friends."

"Yes, sir. Thank you for the information."

As I reassembled the TV, I thought about what Hawk had told me. I had expected them to find a shotgun with Johns' prints on it buried somewhere on the grounds around his house. It verified what I had suspected, even from that first night in his house, when most of the glass from the window had ended up outside the house. That indicated the shotgun blast that tore the window out had been fired from inside—by Doctor Johns.

He had fired that shotgun blast to make us think that someone had tried to kill him.

Was he doing the same thing now, here in Athens?

Was he responsible for the earlier attempts on Sherry and himself?

And most importantly, was he responsible for his wife's disappearance?

There was only one way to find out what the answer was, and that was to confront Johns with what I knew and see what his reaction was.

And there was no time like the present.

THIRTY-ONE

I walked next door and knocked on Johns' door.

"Who is it?" his voice called, and I was sure I detected some nervousness there.

"It's Nick Diamond," I replied.

There was some hesitation, and then the sound of the lock being turned.

"Have you found my wife?" he asked when he opened the door.

"No, not yet."

"Then we have nothing to talk about, Diamond," he said, and attempted to shut the door in my face. I used my shoulder to prevent him from doing so, and brushed by him into the room.

"Now wait just a minute—" he started to bluster, but I ignored him.

"Shut the door," I instructed him, "we have to talk."

"As I said, we have nothing to talk about. Now if you will please leave."

"Let's talk about blowing your own window out

with a sawed-off shotgun to make your government think someone was trying to kill you."

He seemed stunned by my accusation. "What? I don't—"

"What was the plan, Johns? To make the government afraid to send you here? To get them to change their minds about having you attend this meeting?"

"Diamond, you're mad."

"Come on, Johns, stop the playacting. I had the grounds around your house searched. We've found the shotgun with your fingerprints all over it," I told him. "Let's talk about something else, though. Let's talk about you staging a kidnapping with your wife as the victim."

"What?" he asked, looking shocked.

"Sure, you set up the attempt to grab her the other night, when she was with me—and you also set up a phony attack on yourself."

"This is preposterous," he said, stomping around the room.

"Johns, I don't know if you care what happens to your wife, but you'll make it a lot easier to find her if you level with me." I stared at him for a few moments, watching as he paced back and forth nervously. "I'm waiting, Johns," I said, when I felt that he had taken too long without deciding.

"All right, damn you," he snapped. "I did hire some heathen with a rifle to shoot at me. It took me most of that day to find someone, too—someone who wouldn't actually kill me by accident."

"What about those three guys who tried to snatch Sherry from me on the street?" I asked.

"My only aim, Diamond, was to make the government send me home for fear that I would be killed. Having Sherry kidnapped would not accomplish that. Sherry and I may not have the perfect marriage, but I wouldn't deliberately put her in danger."

"For your sake, Johns, I hope that's true."

"What's your angle anyway, Diamond? I know you've been having it off with my wife. Are you in love with her, is that it? Do you love the little sl—"

I poked him in the chest, and he reacted as if I'd pulled a gun on him, backing away with his hands in front of him.

"Don't start that, Doctor. I don't want to hear you badmouthing Sherry. My main concern right now is finding her and finding her safe."

"Fine, then go ahead and do it, but remember that you now no longer work for me, I am no longer paying you."

"That's fine," I said. I wondered if maybe Hawk and I might not have been giving him too much credit in assuming that he might be suspicious of me at this point. He still seemed intent on making me realize that I was fired, as if that was going to send me flying back home.

"I'll be here just long enough to find Sherry, Doctor, and then you can do what you like." I approached him and again he put his hands up in an attempt to avoid another poke in the chest—or worse.

"I warn you, however. If I find out that you're lying to me, and that you knew where she was all along, I'll come back and do much more than just poke you in the chest. I'll cave it in, for you. That's a promise."

"I assure you, Diamond, I know nothing of Sherry's whereabouts. My only desire is to return home and continue my work."

"Yes," I said, staring at him, "and that's probably the biggest part of your problem."

"What problem?" he demanded.

"I don't know if you realize it, Doctor," I said, heading for the door, "but you have a problem relating to other people."

I opened the door and before leaving added, "Maybe you'd better work on that, huh?"

THIRTY-TWO

The ransom demand came the next morning.

A note was left in Doctor Johns' box, and when he was notified that he had a message waiting, he asked the desk to have a bellboy bring it up. Once he read it, he called Robinson right away, who in turn called me.

"We got the note, Nick," he told me. "I'm in the doctor's room."

"I'll be right there," I said. I finished dressing and went next door. The door was already open so I walked in. Robinson was there with Johns, and a couple of his security team.

"Where is it?" I asked.

"Here," he said, handing it to me.

It was written in block letters on cheap bond paper. The handwriting appeared to be deliberately crude. There was only one line: If you want to see your wife again, get $250,000 together by tomorrow afternoon.

"A quarter of a million dollars," I said.

"I don't have that kind of money," Johns said, shaking his head. "This is madness."

"Larry, will the government come up with this ransom?" I asked.

He folded his arms across his chest and took a short glance at the piece of paper in my hand. "Well, I guess they'll just about have to, won't they?"

"Well, they brought Doctor and Mrs. Johns here. I think you'd better make a few calls and try to get that money here by tomorrow morning. I'm sure there'll be another note telling the doctor where to deliver it."

"Me?" Johns asked, looking aghast. "Not me, I'm not walking into somebody's trap."

"You won't be alone, Doctor," Larry told him. "I and some of my men will be right behind you."

"Sure, behind me," Johns said, "where you can't do me any good."

"Uh, Larry," I spoke up, "let's talk about that, okay?"

"Talk about what?"

I motioned for him to come out in the hall with me. "I think I should deliver the money."

"They're going to want Johns to do it," he pointed out. "Whether they really want the money, or they just want to get him out in the open, they're going to want him to be there. If you show up, you might queer the deal."

"Yes, but unless I'm wrong, the government is not going to want to risk Johns getting killed."

"All right, all right, Nick," Larry said. "Let's

work on getting the money, and then we'll see what the instructions are for delivering it. We'll talk about it again then."

"Okay," I said, giving in for the time being. "Let me know what kind of luck you have with the money. I'm going back to my room, and then I'm going downstairs for breakfast."

"Right."

He went back into Johns' room and closed the door. No sooner had I entered my own room than the phone rang; it was Diana Ridgeway.

"Good morning," she said. "I thought perhaps you might like to join me downstairs for breakfast."

"Just you, me, and your security crew?" I asked.

"We'll put them at a separate table," she promised.

"I'll meet you downstairs," I said.

"Super."

I hung up, changed my clothes and went down to have breakfast with the lady of fire and ice.

THIRTY-THREE

"Do they want to frisk me?" I asked her as I sat down opposite her.

John Mount and his very proper group of English security men were eyeing me suspiciously from the next table. I had bid them good morning as I passed their table, but they didn't acknowledge me.

"Oh, they know you're armed, but I think they feel sure that they could prevent you from doing me any harm."

"Well, I'm glad they have confidence in themselves. Have you ordered?"

"No, I thought I would allow you to do that. Order me a very American breakfast."

I ordered scrambled eggs, potatoes, bacon, juice and coffee for both of us.

"Sounds delicious. You're going to make me fat."

"*That,*" I pointed out, "would be doing you serious harm."

"You're sweet."

When breakfast came she proved to have a hearty appetite and I enjoyed watching her eat.

"Did you find the doctor's missing wife?" she asked.

"Unfortunately, no."

"Have you ascertained whether or not she left of her own free will?"

I put down my fork and said, "It would appear not. No one saw her leave the hotel. The security chief, Robinson, had men out looking for her all night."

Around a mouthful of toast and eggs she said, "You have an opinion, don't you?"

"Yes, as a matter of fact, I do," I said, impressed by her ability to read me.

"Want to tell me about it?"

I hesitated a moment, and then decided there was no harm in telling her. "I think she's still somewhere in the hotel."

"That's interesting. Did you check all of the rooms on our floor?"

"All but the Russians' and the Germans'. They refused to allow us access into their rooms."

"That doesn't surprise you, does it?" she asked.

"No."

"Do you think she's in one of those rooms?"

"I don't know."

"How will you find out?"

I shrugged. "One way or another."

"Ooh, that sounds ominous."

"It's not."

"If she was kidnapped, I imagine you should

be hearing from the kidnappers."

"Eventually," I said, choosing not to mention the note already received that morning.

"Will Doctor Johns be attending the meeting tonight?" she asked.

"Yes, of course."

She made a face and said, "That's too bad."

"Why?"

"I don't think you really have to ask me that question," she said, "but I'll answer it, anyway. A few of us were opposed to this meeting of the minds and were pressured into it by our governments, but Dr. Johns seems to be the only one who is actively trying to . . . to sabotage it."

"That's a strong word," I commented.

"And maybe it's the wrong word," she said. She pushed away her empty plate and put some cream in her coffee. "He has no intention of cooperating, he seems intent on insulting all of us every chance he gets, and I think all of that amounts to the same thing—sabotage."

"I know, he's a very easy man to dislike."

"That's an understatement."

I smiled at her and said, "Yeah, knowing the doctor, I guess it is."

"Listen," she said, putting a hand on my arm, "you won't get fired over this, will you? I assume if you were protecting him, you were also supposed to be protecting her."

"That's true," I admitted, "but Doctor Johns hasn't seen fit to blame me for his wife's disappearance."

"Knowing what I do about him, that's surprising."

"Well, we did have an argument, and although he didn't blame me, he did fire me." I don't know why I told her that. It was just a spur of the moment decision.

"Well, now," she said, leaning forward in her chair, "that doesn't mean you'll be leaving Greece, does it?"

"No. I feel a responsibility to Mrs. Johns. I'll be staying until she's found."

"And who will be paying your way?" she asked. "Certainly not Doctor Johns. What about your government? Do you think they will pay to keep you here?"

I laughed, saying, "I doubt it," for her benefit.

"Why don't you work for me, then?" she offered.

"What?"

"Be my personal bodyguard," she said. "You could even move out of your room and into mine. That way you can give me maximum protection."

I stared at her for a few moments, and shook my head in a kind of wonder. "Lady, you sure come on strong," I said. "You're just not my idea of a laboratory type."

"Good," she said, smiling. "That's the impression I've been trying to get across."

"Well, you've done a fine job of it," I said.

I stood up and she said, "How about that job offer?"

"I'll consider it," I promised her.

"I doubt that you'll get a better offer, Nick."

"I'd have to agree with you there, Diana," I answered. "I'd sure have to agree with you there."

THIRTY-FOUR

"You're going to do what?" Larry Robinson asked, staring at me in disbelief.

"Don't look so shocked, Larry," I said. "All I said was that I was going to check out their rooms while you were all at the meeting tonight."

"You're going to break into the German and Russian rooms. Do you know what that could do?"

"Don't tell me about international incidents again, Larry," I replied. "We have to get a look inside those rooms. I have a feeling that Sherry Johns is still in the hotel, somewhere."

"Ah, Nick, she could be anywhere by now," he said.

"No," I insisted, "she's in this hotel, and I'm going to find her."

"What if they leave a security man in their rooms?"

"Well, that'll be for you to find out for me," I explained. "What about the French? Did they have someone in their room?"

"No," he answered, "and the English guys

didn't hear anything that day, so whoever took her didn't come up through the other elevators."

"All right, then. So find out about the Germans and Russians, and then I'll go in and have a look. I want to get it done tonight, before we get the instructions for where to leave the money."

"All right," he agreed, "all right." We were in his room and it was later in the afternoon. He'd had his men out again looking for some sign of her, but they'd come up empty once again.

"I'll try and find out for you."

"Tonight. I'll go downstairs with you. If they haven't left anyone in their rooms, give me the high sign and I'll come back up here."

"Take one of my men with you," he suggested.

"Oh no, I'll do it alone. I can work faster that way. Don't worry about it. What about the money?"

"They're going to fly it in tomorrow on a private jet. It will be delivered up here. I'm going to put a man on the desk downstairs, to see who leaves the note."

"Bad idea."

"Why?" he asked, frowning.

"If they don't see the regular man down there, they won't leave the note. They might not leave it at all. They may just say the hell with it and kill her."

"If they haven't already."

"There's no percentage in killing her now. If we cross them on this, then they might kill her."

"You intend to cross them," he pointed out.

"Once they have the money they may get careless. By the time they discover they've been crossed, they'll have to lead me to her," I said.

"You hope."

"I pray, pal," I corrected him. "I pray."

THIRTY-FIVE

Over Doctor Johns' protests, I accompanied him, Larry and Larry's men down to the meeting.

The security men did another inspection of the main meeting room, this time with Larry. I could hear them talking while they were inside, and when Larry came out he gave me an almost imperceptible shake of the head.

That was the all clear, and I gave him a like nod.

As the five representatives entered the meeting room, I left and went back up to the eighth floor. I remembered the room numbers from Larry's chart and started with Ravinsky's room. It didn't take me very long to check it out, bathroom, closets and all. It was empty, and there was no sign that Sherry had ever been there.

I checked Kruger's room next. Same set up, same results: empty.

Next I had to check the two security rooms, but I'd be a lot more careful about entering them. Larry may not have gotten the straight dope, and I didn't want to walk into a bullet.

I listened at the door of the German security room for a few moments, then went to work on the lock. I had to depend a lot on my instincts in order to enter that room. I left my gun holstered, because if there was someone in there I didn't want a shootout. I didn't want him to kill me, and I sure as hell didn't want to kill him. That, as Larry would say, would be one hell of an international incident.

I pushed the door open and waited a couple of beats before entering. The room appeared empty and there wasn't really anyplace for a man to hide. There were some sleeping bags around, so there were at least two, maybe three men sharing the room. That would be von Klemperer, their security chief, and one or two of this men.

I checked the closet, the bathroom and under the bed. The results were the same as in the other rooms. No Sherry and no sign of her. I even tested the air for the scent of her perfume, but there was none.

The Russian room was next, and I followed the same sequence. Again, the results were the same, and now I was disappointed. I had counted on finding something, some sign of Sherry so that we'd have something to work on, but I had come up empty.

Now all there was for us to do was wait for the instructions about where to deliver the money.

I was no longer in control of the situation, and I wondered who was. Who was standing behind the scenes pulling the strings on this one?

I ran all of the events around in my head, and thought I might just have an answer. I needed to let the man hang himself, though.

Let him hang himself on his own strings.

THIRTY-SIX

The money arrived the following morning at ten; the note came an hour later. It said simply: *Put the money in a flight bag, and go to the Acropolis.*

I had had breakfast again with Diana Ridgeway, and she spent it ranting and raving about Johns' behavior at the meeting the previous night. He had even been more uncooperative, and ruder, if that was possible.

"The others are ready to give it up completely and go back home," she said.

"And you?"

"I'm getting to that point," she admitted.

I regarded her across the table for a long moment and then said, "Don't let him."

"Don't let him what?" she asked.

"Don't let him ruin it," I said. "Don't let him chase you all home. That's what he wants, Diana." I leaned forward to make my point. "Don't let him win."

She examined my face for a long time and then she said, "Thank you, Nick. I won't."

When I returned to my room, Larry had called me and told me that the note had come, and to meet him in the doctor's room.

"Something's wrong," Larry said, staring at the note, frowning.

"What?" I asked.

"The handwriting," he told me, holding the note out, "it's different. Whoever wrote this tried to make it look the same, but it's different."

I looked at it and shook my head. "It looks the same to me."

"Come on, Nick. It's different, anyone can see that," he protested.

"So? Even if it is, all that means is that there are at least two kidnappers."

He shook his head. "I don't like it. I think we should wait."

"Wait? Wait for what?" I asked him.

"I, uh—it just doesn't . . . feel right, you know? You know what I mean, Nick. You have instincts. You have to have them in this business."

"You're right, Larry," I said. "I do have instincts, and mine tell me that everything is going according to plan, both theirs and ours. I think we should do as the note says. Where's the money?"

We were in Johns' room at that point, and he was sitting on the couch, trying to pretend that nothing that was going on involved him.

"The money is in my room," Larry said, "but we have to talk about this, Nick."

"Okay, so let's talk," I said. "Meanwhile, we can send one of your men out to get a flight bag."

"Let's talk, first."

"Whatever you say," I replied.

We left Johns' room and went back to Larry's.

"I don't like the way it feels, Nick," he said, opening the door.

"Why, Larry?"

"I don't know why," he said, "I can't tell you why, I can only tell you that it feels . . . wrong. It feels . . . bad, somehow," he tried to explain.

"Look, Larry," I said sitting on the couch. "You're in charge of this operation. You don't like the way it feels, you do what you think is best."

"And what are you going to do?" he asked.

"I'm going to do what I think is best . . . for Sherry Johns," I told him.

"And I have to do what I think is best for our government, Nick. *Our* government, remember?"

I held my hands up and said, "Do what you have to do."

"Goddamnit, Nick!"

"Don't let me influence you."

"Nick, you know I respect your opinions," he said.

"And I respect yours, Larry, but we respect our own even more. We've got to do what we think is right. I think it's right to get Sherry Johns out of a situation she has no business being in."

"We have to keep our government out of a situation they have no business being in," he said. "That's our responsibility."

"Look, I was sent here in an unofficial capacity to work as Doctor Johns' private bodyguard. He fired me, so my job is done."

"That's bullshit. You're playing word games. You work for the government, just like me."

"Not just like you, Larry," I pointed out. "You're what they call regular army. I'm special services."

"So?"

"This is a regular army operation. I was here as a favor, sort of on loan, but I'm as good as blown." I was stretching the truth now. "Johns knows something is up, so he's fired me. That's it, I'm done!"

He put his hands on his hips and stared at the wall behind me. He knew it was futile to argue with me any further. "The note," he said to me, trying again anyway.

"What about it?" I asked.

"It doesn't say when?"

"So, whoever takes the money goes to the Acropolis and spends the day there. There's enough there to keep him busy until contact is made."

"Whoever?" he asked. "I thought you said you wanted to take the money?"

"I've changed my mind. I think Johns should do it, and I think you and a couple of your men should trail him."

His eyebrows went up and he said, "That's a switch. Why the change of heart?"

"I have a hunch."

He waited for me to go on, and when I didn't he said, "Do you want to let me in on it?"

"I have a hunch that while you and Johns are at the Acropolis, they're going to try and get Sherry out of the hotel. I want to watch and be ready for them when they do."

"You've still got that idea that she's in this hotel," he said.

"I've still got it," I replied, "until somebody proves me wrong. While you and the doctor are at the Acropolis, I'll be sitting in the lobby . . . waiting."

"Okay," he said after a moment, "you win, Nick. I'll play it your way, but if nothing happens, you play it my way later on."

"You got a deal, Larry," I said, getting up. "I'll see you later on."

THIRTY-SEVEN

I sat and waited while Johns, Larry and two of his men went to visit the Acropolis. If they came back and told me that the connection had been made, and that the money had passed hands, then I'd know I was right.

There was another way I'd know too, though, and that was what I was waiting for now. I wasn't waiting in the lobby, as I had told Larry I would be, but in his room. I was watching the needle on his listening device monitor, waiting for it to jump. Nobody was supposed to be in Johns' room, but when the needle jumped, I'd know I was right.

I was hoping the needle wouldn't jump, but when it did, I would be ready.

Some of it was obvious, now. Johns had admitted as much. There were no honest attempts made on his life. Both of the attempts had been manufactured by him in a vain attempt to get the American government to first change their minds about sending him to Athens, and then once he was in Athens, to change their minds and bring him back home. Neither had worked, but in the meantime, someone else had set a plan into motion . . . to do what? What was the point of trying to grab Sherry Johns, and then finally succeeding in doing so?

I thought that the whole point was money, a quarter of a million dollars. Whether it came from Johns or the American government, the kidnappers didn't care, as long as they got it.

If Johns had had that much money, I seriously wondered if he would have been willing to part with it. The government, on the other hand, would come up with it to either keep him happy, or keep the whole affair out of the headlines. They didn't want any attention drawn to this summit meeting. It was supposed to be run on the Q-T, and nothing must interfere with that.

So again, it was for Johns' safety as much as anything else that the United States had flown a quarter of a million dollars to Athens on a moment's notice.

They put a high price on Johns' life, but to me he wasn't worth a dollar. He wasn't worth the energy it took to protect him, and he was probably doing more harm than good in Athens.

I was convinced that Johns had nothing to do with Sherry's disappearance. It had to be someone who knew who she was, though, and who knew about the summit meeting, knew that somebody would come up with the money to keep the whole thing quiet.

It was somebody who was involved with the meeting, somebody in the hotel.

Was it the English, the French, the Germans or the Russians? Would they need a quarter of a million dollars? That was a drop in the bucket of any of their treasuries.

If not a country, then who?

An individual, but which one?

If a member of any of the other security teams wanted to extort a half a million dollars, why pick the wife of an American doctor? Why not snatch one of their own and ransom the person to their own country?

I was so attuned to that needle that the moment it jumped I snapped out of my reverie. It didn't even jump that much, just enough to indicate that someone was moving around in Doctor Johns' room.

I went to the door and opened it about an inch, just so I could see down the hall. I had a couple of hunches about who would come walking out of that room, and I intended to tail them. When someone did come out of the room, though, I was caught completely off guard.

It was Sherry Johns.

THIRTY-EIGHT

Despite the black wig and dark glasses, I knew it was her. I could tell simply by the way she moved, the way she walked.

I was surprised, but not so surprised that I couldn't follow her. If she had come out of that room sans wig and glasses, I might have approached her, I might have assumed that the connection had been made and that she had been set free.

The wig and glasses, though, indicated that everything was not on the up and up, here. Sherry Johns had snatched herself, or so it seemed, and she undoubtedly had not done so alone.

Instead of walking toward me and the nearby elevator, she went the other way to use the elevator at the other end of the floor. When she turned the corner I left the room, and sprinted down the hall. I peered around and saw her press the elevator call button. I waited until the car arrived and she got in, and then I sprinted toward the elevator, hoping I'd be in time to see what floor she got off.

When I reached the elevator bank, the indicator showed that the car had stopped on two. After that it passed the mezzanine between two and one and went directly to the main floor.

I felt pretty certain that she had gotten off on two. There was too much of a chance that she would be seen and recognized in the lobby. She had obviously been keeping herself under wraps since her "disappearance," but then there must have been something in her room that she wanted, and now she wasn't missing anymore.

At least, as far as I was concerned, she wasn't. She was in the hotel, as I had suspected, somewhere on the second floor.

I needed someone who could tell me which room, though.

I went down to the main floor and stopped at the desk.

"Can I help you, sir?" the clerk asked in English.

"Yes. I'd like to speak to the bell captain," I said.

"Certainly, sir. If you will wait in the lounge, I will have him come to you."

Very cooperative and polite, the Greeks. That would make it easier.

I had to wait only a few minutes and then a man in his early forties approached me and said, "*Herete*," which means "hello" and "goodbye," depending on how you use it. "You are looking for me, sir?" he asked.

"Are you the bell captain?" I asked.

"I am."

I stood up and extended my hand to him. He hesitated, then shook hands with me, and a five hundred drachma note changed hands.

"I do not understand."

"I need a bellboy who knows the second floor," I told him. "There's one of those in it for him, and another in it for you."

"*Neh*," he said simply, meaning "yes." "Wait here."

"*Efharisto*," I said, thanking him.

He returned a few moments later with a boy about nineteen or so, who was eyeing me hungrily. No doubt he had been told that I was anxious to give him some money, and he was eager to please. I shook hands with the bell captain again, and passed him another five hundred drachma note.

"*Efharisto*," he said, and withdrew, leaving me and the young man alone.

I approached the bellboy and stuffed a green five hundred drachma note into his jacket pocket. "There is a lady on the second floor whose acquaintance I would like to make," I said.

"A lady?" he asked. "What does she look like?"

I described Sherry as best I could, adding the dark wig and the glasses. His eyes lit up and I knew that he knew who I meant.

"A very pretty lady, sir," he said.

I showed him a couple of red one hundred drachma notes and then hid them in my fist.

"She is in room 205, sir. She does not come out,

much," he said, eyeing my closed hand.

"*Efharisto*," I said, and shook hands with him, passing him the red notes.

THIRTY-NINE

It was a good evening's work. I had accomplished two things. I had found Sherry Johns and I'd stopped feeling sorry for her. She was obviously very well able to take care of herself. She was involved in her own kidnapping, and she might even be the brains of the operation. That still remained to be seen.

My first thought was to go up to the second floor and pay her a visit, but I decided against it. I didn't want to spook her and blow my chance at finding out who her partner, or partners were.

I went to the front desk and the desk clerk asked once again if he could help me. I hit him with a question that I had neglected to ask the bellboy, but I didn't ask it straight out.

"I was wondering if I would be able to change my room?" I asked him.

He looked alarmed. "Is your room not satisfactory, sir?"

"No, no, it's very satisfactory. It's just that I'm a little superstitious."

"Superstitious."

"Yes, about a certain number," I explained. "205."

"205?" he asked me, looking at me like I was some kind of a crazy American.

"That's right."

"I will check for you," he said.

He checked his register, and then began to shake his head sadly.

"I am sorry, sir, but that room is taken."

"Oh, really? How long do you think it will be taken for?"

"I really don't know, sir. Miss Jones only registered yesterday. She did not say how long she would be staying."

"I see. Well, thank you, anyway."

"You're very welcome, sir. I hope you enjoy the remainder of your stay."

"Oh, it's getting better all ready," I assured him.

"Jones." Not only was it a common name, but it was very close to her real name of "Johns."

For a smart girl, she was showing remarkably little imagination.

FORTY

I was seated in the lobby when Larry came back with Doctor Johns, two of his men—and no money!

"How'd it go?" I asked, even though I saw that they no longer had the bag of money.

"Contact was made," Larry said, looking as if he were trying to suppress excitement.

"The bag was taken from my hand in the museum," Johns added. "By the time I turned to see who it was, they were gone."

"Any of your people get a look?" I asked Larry.

He gave me a grim shake of his head. "I don't know how they could have done it, Nick, I really don't," he said. "We were all over the doctor like a second skin and they still got away with it."

"You didn't lose him at all?" I asked.

"Well," he said, hesitantly, "Maybe just for a couple of seconds . . ."

"And that's when they made their move," I finished.

He nodded dejectedly and said, "That's the way it seems."

"All right, Larry," I told him, "I guess there was nothing you could do about it. They probably had you spotted all the way."

"I would like to protest the handling of this entire affair," Johns said suddenly. "I believe that my life was endangered, today." He went on, "and needlessly, I might add—"

"Doctor," Larry said tiredly, "please shut up."

It was phrased like a request, but the tone behind it clearly implied something else, so Johns lapsed into silence.

"Why don't we get him back to his room," I suggested, "and then we can decide what we're going to do."

"Right," Larry agreed.

We went up in the elevator and escorted the doctor back to his room.

"Dave," Larry said to one of his men, "you and Johnson stay in the room with the doctor. We don't want to take any chances at this point in the game."

"Yes, sir," Dave replied, and both men remained with the doctor, while Robinson and I returned to his room.

At least, I started for Larry's room with him, but I decided to make a detour.

"Larry, I'll be with you in a minute. Why don't you order a bottle of bourbon sent up to the room. This is liable to be a long, dry session, all right?"

"Sure, Nick. Uh, where are you going?"

"I've just got something I'd like to check on, that's all. I'll be right with you."

He nodded and I watched as he walked down to his room and disappeared inside. I turned and walked to the other end of the hall, then made a right and continued on until I came to Diana Ridgeway's room.

When she answered my knock she looked pleased to see me.

"Well," she said, "have you decided to accept my offer, after all?"

"May I come in?" I asked.

"Of course," she replied, backing away. She was wearing a sheer dressing gown, and her body moved easily underneath, unencumbered by any additional clothing.

As I entered I shut the door behind me and said, "I am here about your offer, in a way."

"Oh, in what way?" she asked.

"I have a counter offer," I explained, "that I hope you'll be interested in . . ."

FORTY-ONE

After a short meeting with Diana Ridgeway, at which we both came to a mutual understanding, I left her room and headed back around to Larry Robinson's room.

He answered my knock with a freshly opened bottle of bourbon in his hand.

"Come on in," he said, waving it, "you're just in time."

I entered and closed the door behind me.

"Grab a glass, Nick," he said, pouring himself a generous portion of bourbon, "we're celebrating Larry Robinson's royal fuck up!"

"Don't be so hard on yourself, Larry," I told him, taking the bottle from him and making my own drink.

"Why not?" he asked. "It'll be good practice for what's going to happen to me when we get back to Washington. Wait until they go over the way I handled this whole thing. I cost the government a ~arter of a million dollars, and we didn't even get ~ns back."

"Maybe they'll let her go, now that they have the money," I suggested.

"You and I know that ain't going to happen," he said, reaching for the bottle again. I hadn't even noticed that he'd finished the first drink.

I handed it to him and said, "Anything can happen."

"Sure," he said, "keep a stiff upper lip, as our British friends say, right?" I found that remark to be both ironic and prophetic.

"Larry," I said, suddenly unwilling to play any more games, "you're not going to do a drunk act on me, are you?"

"*Hmm*?" he asked, with his mouth in his glass, staring comically at me from over it.

"You're planning to do the poor, drunk sorry-for-himself agent act, aren't you?" I asked. "I don't think we need that, do you?"

"What are you talking about?" he demanded.

"I'm sure you really feel like celebrating the fact that everything went right, don't you?" I asked.

"Nick, I think you're the one who's drunk, boy," he replied, "and off one little drink, too."

"Let's drop the dumb act, too, okay?" I said, putting my drink down.

"I'll tell you what," he said. "If you've got something you want to say, why don't you just spit it out?"

"Sure," I agreed. "You got your money, you should be as happy as a pig in shit."

"My money?" he asked. "Let me get this

straight, pal. You think I took the money?"

"You and your partner," I added.

"My partner?" he asked. "And who might that be?"

"The dark haired woman down in room two-oh-five, Larry," I answered. "You know, Sherry Johns."

"Shit," he said, producing his gun. "Goddamn you, Nick!" It was the calmest exclamation of disgust I had ever heard uttered.

"Sorry, Larry. Did I mess something up?"

"How did you know?" he asked. "How the hell did you know?"

I eyed his gun calmly and said, "Because I've worked with you before, Larry. I know you're good, and this whole security thing was so badly handled that it was hard for me to believe that you were in charge."

"Come on," he said. "What else?"

"Oh, little things, but most of all it was the note, the one that was delivered today."

"What about it?"

"You were right," I said, "it wasn't written by the same person, and that threw you off, didn't it? Because the first note was written by Sherry herself, and she probably had a bellboy deliver it to the desk. The second note," I went on, "the second note was written by me."

"By you?" he asked, in surprise.

"Yep. Well, actually, mine was the third note. This one," I said, taking a folded piece of paper out of my pocket, "this one is the second note, written by Sherry."

I handed it to him and he read it. I had picked up the real note much earlier in the morning, and replaced it with one of my own. The real note had an entirely different place for the drop to be made, a place no doubt agreed upon by Larry and Sherry. When he saw my note, though, he must have thought that Sherry had changed her mind. He didn't have time to check with her, so he set up a quick snatch for the Acropolis, after arguing with me first about not liking the way the note felt. That much was true, but in the end he decided to work it out, anyway, and that was when I knew it was him.

"Where's the money, Larry?" I asked him. "Who made the pickup from Johns?"

"Nobody," he said. "Stand up, Nick."

"We going downstairs to visit with your partner?" I asked, rising.

"Shut up. Take out your gun with two fingers of your left hand, then drop that hideaway knife you carry on your wrist. Make a move I don't like and I'll finish you off right here."

"Take it easy, Larry," I said. "There's no point in getting nervous this late in the game . . . or have you been nervous all along?"

"Shut up."

I dropped Wilhelmina and Hugo onto the floor and kept talking. "After all, old pal, this is your first time on the wrong side of the fence, isn't it?"

"Yeah," he answered, "as a matter of fact, it is, but it's been a long time coming. First they assign me to babysit that shithead Johns, and then they send you along to watch me. You didn't think I swallowed that bullshit about you being Johns' personal bodyguard, did you? They sent you to watch me."

"So you decided to rip off the United States government because your feelings were hurt?"

"Because I had it coming," he said. "I had the quarter million coming, and more. They fucked me over more than once, Nick, and I ain't going to be their patsy anymore. Let's move out of the room, now. My gun will be in my pocket and my hand will be on it, so don't make any moves I don't tell you to. Got it?"

"I've got it, Larry."

"Let's go, out the door and to the elevator."

"Up or down?" I asked.

"Don't get smart!"

Larry Robinson fit the mold I had set for the kidnapper. He was involved with the summit meeting, he knew the entire setup, and he was smart enough to have planned it. I didn't think he had it planned right from the beginning, though, but meeting Johns and finding out that I was going to be along for the duration had pushed him over the edge. Obviously, he had been feeling that he hadn't been getting his just due for a long time now, and he'd decided that this was the time to make a score and get out.

He had set up the phony grab on Sherry that first

night on the street, probably just hiring three Greek workers to make a show of it. When did he get Sherry to agree to go in on it, though? Before or after that?

Well, I'd be able to ask her about it as soon as we got to room 205.

FORTY-TWO

"Why did you bring him along?" Sherry Johns demanded when we entered the room. Larry had used his key to get in.

"He figured it out," he explained.

She looked at me with what appeared to be genuine sadness and said, "I'm sorry, Nick."

"Don't be sorry," Larry told her. "I told you this might happen. I told you he was smart, and goddamnit, I told you not to sleep with him—"

"Don't start that," she said.

"No," he agreed, "I won't start that. It's too late for recriminations."

"When did he rope you into this, Sherry? Before or after the incident in the street?"

She looked at Larry, as if to ask if she should answer, but he just shrugged and kept his gun on me.

"After that, Nick. I think that Larry surmised that I was as unhappy in my situation as he was in his, and when he approached me with his plan, I figured why not? I told you I couldn't go back to the chorus line, and my share of a quarter of a million dollars will keep me off."

"Why only a quarter of a million, Larry?" I asked.

"I didn't want to make waves, ask too much. I figured a quarter million wouldn't matter that much to the United States government, and I guess I was right."

"So where's the money?" I asked.

"Stashed," he answered, "where I can get at it, tomorrow, next week, or next month."

"Oh, I get it. Sherry here was going to make a reappearance sometime today with a phony story about being blindfolded for the last few days, and then released. Then you could finish up the meeting, and either pick up the money before you left, or come back and get it."

"That's the plan."

"And it probably would have worked, too, except that now you have to kill me."

"So what?" Larry said. "As far as anyone at this meeting knows, you're just a hired American body-guard. If you disappear, who's going to worry? Especially when they find out that you were fired after Mrs. Johns disappeared. They'll just assume that you went back to the States."

"And what about Washington?" I asked.

"They've lost agents before, Nick. You won't be the first to disappear without a trace."

"You're adaptable, Larry, I'll give you that," I said. "Especially after today."

"What does he mean?" Sherry asked.

"He replaced your note with a note of his own,"

he explained, "saying that the drop would be made at the Acropolis."

"But that wasn't what we planned," she said.

"I know that," Larry replied sharply, "but I had no time to check with you, and I had to act fast, so we—I made the drop, anyway."

"And that's how he knew it was you," she said. "If it wasn't, no one would have been at the Acropolis and you would have come back with the money."

"As I said," Larry remarked, "he's smart."

"I'm smart enough to know one thing, Sherry," I spoke up.

"What?" she asked.

"That a two way split of a quarter of a million dollars isn't quite enough for Larry's purposes."

"Shut up," Larry said.

"What do you mean?" she asked.

"Larry asked for a quarter of a million because it's not too high a figure for the government to have balked at, but it's enough for one person to live on, fairly comfortably." I paused and then said it again for emphasis. "One person, Sherry."

"Larry—"

"Shut up," he told her now.

"See, he's going to kill us both, only he'll let them find your body, and everyone will assume that the kidnappers killed you. Hell, they might even assume that I was the kidnapper, since I'm slated to disappear. It'll all be very neat."

"Larry, what's he saying?" she demanded, looking at Robinson, nervously.

"Shut up, Sherry," he told her. He looked around the room, then went to the couch and picked up a cushion that was large enough to act as an effective silencer.

"Larry, you promised," she was telling him. "We had plans, remember, baby? We were going to be together?"

"Sure, baby, sure," he said. "I've got plans, all right, but they don't include you."

He leveled the gun at her and was about to fire when I said, "Who's that?"

"Who's what?" he asked.

"I thought I heard a knock on the door," I said, loudly.

He gave me a look that said who-are-you-trying-to-kid.

"Nice try, Nick."

At that point there was a knock on the door.

"Shit," Larry snapped. He looked at Sherry and asked her, "Did you order anything from room service?"

Before she answered she looked at me nervously and I nodded slowly.

"Oh, yes, I d-did," she stammered.

"Get rid of them," he said, motioning with the gun for her to go to the door.

She walked to the door, which put her within arm's reach of me, and called out, "Who is it?"

"Room service," a voice replied.

"I-I've changed my mind," she called out. "I don't want room service, now."

There was no reply from the other side of the

door, so I moved quickly toward the door and said, "Oh, hell, let's let them in."

"Nick—" Larry shouted, but my hand was on the knob already, and as I turned it the door swung open.

Robinson, expecting a bellboy, didn't quite know what to do. He didn't want to have a dead bellboy on his hands, because that might make the body count too unmanageable, so he made a snap decision and put the gun behind his back.

As the door opened he found himself looking down the gun barrels of the Englishman, John Mount, and two of his men.

"We have your order, sir," Mount said, with somewhat uncharacteristic humor.

Larry's eyes snapped to me and I could see him considering it.

"It's not worth it, Larry," I said to him. "Besides, I don't think you really want to kill me, anyway. Give it up, pal. It's over."

He thought it over one more time, and then I heard his gun hit the floor behind him with a dull thud.

FORTY-THREE

I called Johns' room and told Dave, who answered the phone, to bring Johns to room 205. When they arrived they took everything in with puzzled glances as they saw the English security crew holding Robinson at gunpoint.

I explained everything to them rather quickly, and the one called Dave took control rather nicely. He was young and eager, which helped. He went to the phone and called for more men, and when they arrived they escorted both Sherry and Larry Robinson from the room. Robinson did not resist at all, and neither did Sherry Johns. She gave me a lingering look as she was marched from the room, but as I no longer felt sorry for her, I ignored it.

I thanked John Mount and his men, and told him to extend my thanks also to Diana Ridgeway. When the crowd was gone there was only me and Doctor Lucas Johns, alone in room 205.

"Shocking," he said, shaking his head. "An American agent, and my wife, plotting against me and my country. I've always said that the government men—"

I figured what the hell, I had enough on him to keep him in line, so I finally hauled off and slugged him on the point of the jaw, hitting him just hard enough to satisfy myself without knocking him unconscious. He sat down in the middle of the floor and stared up at me with a bloody lip.

"Y-you hit me?"

"And if you get up before I tell you to, I'm going to hit you again, Doctor," I told him. "Don't you make noises to me about somebody plotting against *your* country," I told him. "You're just as guilty as they are."

"W-what do you mean?"

"I'll tell you exactly what I mean," I said, "and I'm not just talking about faking attempts on your life. You were part of their plot to defraud the government of a quarter of a million dollars."

"I swear, Diamond," he said, "I had no intention of taking a cent of that money."

"No, I know you didn't," I told him. "You were giving them your cooperation because you thought that this kidnapping episode would finally get you sent home, where you could continue your work. For that, you didn't mind helping Robinson get his hands on a quarter of a million bucks, while throwing your wife in for good measure. What you didn't know was that Robinson intended to kill your wife."

"Kill her?" he asked with a shocked look on his face.

"And maybe you, too, for all I know," I added, and he started to look sick. I didn't know what Larry Robinson had intended for Doctor Johns, although I didn't see how he could leave the doctor alive once the body of Sherry Johns was found.

That didn't matter now, though. I knew Johns was involved for three reasons. He had already tried to put one over on the government twice, so I knew he wouldn't hesitate to do so a third time, especially if he thought that the third time would be the proverbial charm.

Then there was the fact that even though Larry Robinson knew that the note I had written had not been written by Sherry Johns, he went along with the instructions on it. That meant that there had to be a third person involved, since he had obviously assumed that a third person had written the note, that third person being Doctor Johns. I didn't know if they'd had an opportunity to exchange notes at the Acropolis, although I doubted it, what with the other American security men around.

My third reason was the fact that Larry had not come back with the money, but said that it had been stashed. It wouldn't have been very hard for him to attract the attention of his men long enough for Johns to have hidden the money somewhere in the Acropolis. And it had to be Johns, because there was no one else Larry could have brought into his plan. I doubted that he wanted to involve any of his men or even risk approaching one of them, and Johns had a built-in reason for wanting to go along. He must have approached Johns sometime just before they faked the kidnapping, which in itself had been simple enough. Sherry had simply left my room, had gone either to the second floor room or to Larry Robinson's room, disguised herself and then had gone downstairs to re-register as the dark-haired lady.

I had the feeling that the latter applied, that while I was checking empty rooms on the eighth floor, she had been hiding in the only room, other than those belonging to the Russians and Germans, that hadn't been searched.

Larry Robinson's room.

"You can get up now, Doctor," I told him.

He got unsteadily to his feet, eyeing me warily lest I try to hit him again.

"I think it's safe to say that I saved your life, Doctor, which is what you hired me to do in the first place, isn't it?" I asked.

He nodded jerkily.

"All right, then. Here's what I want you to do. Tonight, and all the rest of the nights of this meeting, you will attend the sessions, be cordial to all concerned and contribute to the proceedings. Also, tomorrow morning, you and I will go to the Acropolis and you can show me where you hid that flight bag filled with funny money."

"F-funny money?" he asked. "I don't understand."

"Well, you didn't think I would let my government risk a quarter of a million dollars of their money when I knew all along that the kidnapping was a phony, did you?" I asked.

"You mean, all that money is . . . counterfeit?"

"That's correct, Doctor. Imagine what Larry Robinson would have thought when he discovered that."

He thought about it a moment, then said, "He probably would have thought that I switched bags on him. But where would I get that much counterfeit—"

"That wouldn't matter, Doctor."

"He would have killed me," he said, suddenly looking sick again.

"If he hadn't already killed you, remember? So I guess you can say that I saved your life twice, couldn't you?"

"I-I suppose so."

"So in exchange for my not informing the United States government of your part in attempting to extort a quarter of a million dollars from them, you will try your utmost to make this summit meeting as successful as possible, won't you?" I asked.

Looking very much the picture of a beaten man, he replied, "Yes, I will."

"Fine. Let's go back to your room so you can get ready for tonight's session."

As we started from the room, I said, "Oh yes, Doctor, one more thing."

"Yes?"

I smiled at him and said, "I quit."

FORTY-FOUR

What I had told Johns about the money being counterfeit had been totally true. I had contacted David Hawk last night and instructed him—that is, I suggested—that he intervene with General Davies and make sure that a quarter of a million dollars of Federally confiscated counterfeit money be sent to Athens instead of real money.

Larry Robinson's erratic behavior and sloppy handling of security had been bothering me ever since my arrival in Athens. When I had finally decided that someone connected with the summit meetings was involved with everything that was going on, he was the logical choice.

After Doctor Johns had left for the night's session in the company of the remaining American security men, I contacted Hawk once again and related the evening's events to him.

"Then everything went according to your plan, N3," he said, satisfied.

I did not tell him that there was also a lot of luck involved, but simply said, "Yes sir, it did."

"Excellent. No harm has come to Doctor Johns?"

"None," I said, also neglecting to mention the beautiful bruise he was sporting on the point of his chin.

"Very good," he replied. "You don't look very happy, N3. Are there any further problems?"

"Not really, sir. It's just that I don't approve of letting Doctor Johns off scot free."

I had anticipated some sort of reprisal against the doctor just for his phony attempts on his life. Now, after he had also been involved in attempted extortion, the government still intended to let him off with not even a slap on the wrist.

"Doctor Johns' work is very important to this country, Nick," Hawk told me. "Indeed, perhaps even to the world."

"It irks me to think that this ill-mannered, pompous, overbearing, insensitive . . . he as much as drove his wife right into Larry Robinson's scheme," I said. "If he had been some kind of a husband to her, she might not have been so vulnerable to Robinson's plan."

"That's neither here nor there as far as the government is concerned, Nick," he informed me.

"I know that, sir, but all that does is make the government almost as insensitive as he is."

"I think perhaps you need a vacation, Nick," Hawk said to me.

I looked at him in surprise.

"That's not like you at all, sir," I said suspiciously.

"That's odd," he said. "I was just having the same thoughts about you, N3."

I smiled at my crafty superior and said, "I get your drift, sir."

"I rather thought you would," he observed.

"Do you want me back in Washington right away, sir?" I asked him.

"Do you think that the security men there can handle Doctor Johns without you?" he asked.

"Oh, I'm certain they can, sir. The doctor and I have come to an agreement, which I think he will abide by—for a while, anyway." Until he thought about it and realized his own worth to the United States government. I had no doubt that, sooner or later, he'd figure it out and return to his normal, insulting, ill-mannered self.

"Then why would you want to stay?" Hawk asked.

"Well," I said, "I've had a job offer here, now that I am no longer working for Doctor Johns as Nick Diamond, private eye."

"A job offer?" Hawk asked. "Are you thinking about leaving AXE, Nick?"

"No, no, it's nothing like that, sir," I said, thinking about Diana Ridgeway. "No, I think what it amounts to, sir," I explained, "is simply a little something on the side."

DON'T MISS THE NEXT NEW NICK CARTER SPY THRILLER

THE OUTBACK GHOSTS

The sun sank and some of the heat of the summer day vanished. Under the cover of deepening twilight, I started down the alley behind the house. At the back of the house stood large trash bins overflowing with refuse. They provided cover as I worked my way forward. A cleared patch of almost ten feet between my position and the back door leading into the kitchen was protected by a motion sensor.

I dropped to my belly and began inching forward, sticking to shadows, moving so slowly my progress seemed nonexistent. But almost twenty minutes later, my outstretched hand brushed against the foundations of the house. No alarm had warned of my approach.

Still moving slower than molasses on a cold day, I snaked upright and peered into a window into a dining room. Three men and a woman sat at a table playing cards. From the money on the table I guessed at poker. Even the most diligent of KGB agents can be corrupted with Western ways.

I slid along the wall, safer now than I had been out in the open stretch. The motion sensors would be directed outward; I moved under their beam. A second window into the kitchen revealed another pair of agents—a man and a woman. From the way they went at it so hot and heavy, it would take them several minutes to recover if I went in.

So I did.

The man had his pants down—literally—when I walked into the kitchen. He turned. His face contorted into anger then went slack as I jabbed hard into his solar plexus. He went out like a light. The woman sprawled back on the kitchen table reacted faster than I would have thought possible. Maybe she had been faking her passion.

At any rate, I had to move fast. Hugo pinned her wrist to the wooden table as she reached for a Tokorov 7.65mm automatic.

"*Aiieee!*" she shrieked, as pain flooded her body. There wasn't a second outcry. My knuckles pushed hard into her carotid arteries. In less than a minute she was out cold. I retrieved Hugo and hefted the small Russian automatic. No sense using Wilhelmina's bullets if the KGB supplied ammo for me. I hurried to the door to listen. If the woman's brief outcry had been heard, I might be up to my ears in boiling mad KGB agents.

I strained to hear the conversation going on among the card players in the next room. I almost laughed when I caught the drift of what they were saying. The man I'd knocked out was the local bureau chief and the woman was a new agent—one more intent on getting ahead in KGB ranks than anything else. The card players made crude jokes about how much fun the woman was actually having and how much she was faking.

Glancing back, I made sure both the bureau chief and his mistress were still out cold. Then I moved.

"One word and you're dead," I said quietly to the card players. Four against one is lousy odds, even when the one held an automatic. And the foursome knew it. Even as I told them to stay quiet, I shifted the pistol to my left hand and sent Hugo directly into the windpipe of the man farthest from me.

That reduced my odds, gave the KGB agents something else to think about for a second and permitted me to cross the room. A karate chop to the throat took out the woman. A kick to the groin doubled over one of the two remaining men. And the last man wasn't about to argue now—the Tokorov pointed directly for his head.

"There's no need to shoot," he said softly. Only a slight tremor in his voice betrayed the intense emotion he felt.

"Tie them up. Now. Start with him." I indicated the man groaning and clutching his groin. When that was done, I pointed toward the woman. The third man presented no problem to anyone any more. He was quite dead. I stripped all of them of their weapons. The pile was large enough for me to open my own pawn shop back in the States. After I'd tied my unwilling helper and gagged all three of the living, I stuffed the spare ammo and clips into my jacket pocket and went off in search of anyone else in the house.

Marian had thought there might be eight. I'd taken six out of the game.

His count was accurate. I decked one man coming out of the john. But the way he thrashed about as he fell overturned a lamp and the table under it. The eighth man came out of a bedroom with guns blazing.

I dodged but still felt a hot crease across my shoulders. Nothing too bad, but enough to let me know how close I'd come to death on my one-man grandstanding play. The KGB agent tried to reach his fallen comrade. I held him back with a few well-placed shots. But this firefight couldn't go on too long. Even in a neighborhood like this, prolonged gunfire will draw police—and crowds.

"Give it up," I called out in Russian. "There are too many of us. We have you!"

He fired with both guns again.

—From THE OUTBACK GHOSTS
A New Nick Carter Spy Thriller
From Ace Charter In March

☐ 03128-5	**ASSASSINATION BRIGADE**	$2.25
☐ 05381-5	**BEIRUT INCIDENT**	$2.25
☐ 09028-1	**THE CAIRO MAFIA**	$2.50
☐ 09173-3	**CARNIVAL FOR KILLING**	$2.25
☐ 09274-8	**CAULDRON OF HELL**	$2.50
☐ 10351-0	**CHESSMASTER**	$2.50
☐ 13573-0	**THE DAMOCLES THREAT**	$2.50
☐ 13935-3	**DAY OF THE DINGO**	$1.95
☐ 14172-2	**THE DEATH STAR AFFAIR**	$2.50
☐ 14169-2	**DEATHLIGHT**	$2.50
☐ 14399-7	**THE DEVIL'S DOZEN**	$2.50
☐ 15244-9	**THE DOMINICAN AFFAIR**	$2.50

Available at your local bookstore or return this form to:

 ACE CHARTER BOOKS
P.O. Box 400, Kirkwood, N.Y. 13795

Please send me the titles checked above. I enclose _____ .
Include 75¢ for postage and handling if one book is ordered; 50¢ per book for
two to five. If six or more are ordered, postage is free. California, Illinois, New
York and Tennessee residents please add sales tax.

NAME _____

ADDRESS _____

CITY_____ STATE ZIP_____

Allow six weeks for delivery.

A8

NICK CARTER

☐ 15870-1	**DOOMSDAY SPORE**	$1.75
☐ 17014-5	**THE DUBROVNIK MASSACRE**	$2.25
☐ 18124-4	**EARTH SHAKER**	$2.50
☐ 29782-X	**THE GOLDEN BULL**	$2.25
☐ 34909-9	**THE HUMAN TIME BOMB**	$2.25
☐ 34999-4	**THE HUNTER**	$2.50
☐ 35868-3	**THE INCA DEATH SQUAD**	$2.50
☐ 35881-0	**THE ISRAELI CONNECTION**	$2.50
☐ 43201-8	**KATMANDU CONTRACT**	$2.25
☐ 47183-8	**THE LAST SAMURAI**	$2.50
☐ 58866-2	**NORWEGIAN TYPHOON**	$2.50
☐ 64053-2	**THE OMEGA TERROR**	$1.95
☐ 63400-1	**OPERATION: McMURDO SOUND**	$2.50
☐ 64426-0	**THE OUSTER CONSPIRACY**	$2.25

Available at your local bookstore or return this form to:

 ACE CHARTER BOOKS
P.O. Box 400, Kirkwood, N.Y. 13795

Please send me the titles checked above. I enclose _____.
Include 75¢ for postage and handling if one book is ordered; 50¢ per book for
two to five. If six or more are ordered, postage is free. California, Illinois, New
York and Tennessee residents please add sales tax.

NAME _____

ADDRESS _____

CITY_____ STATE ZIP_____

Allow six weeks for delivery.